ULYSSES MOORE

THE ISLE OF MASKS

MOORE

SCHOLASTIC INC.

New York   Toronto   London   Auckland   Sydney
Mexico City   New Delhi   Hong Kong   Buenos Aires

ISBN-13: 978-0-439-77671-4
ISBN-10: 0-439-77671-6

Copyright © 2006 by Edizioni Piemme S.p.A., via G. del Carretto 10, 15033 Casale Monferrato (AL), Italia.
English translation copyright © 2006 by Edizioni Piemme S.p.A.

Illustrations by Iacopo Bruno

Special thanks to James Preller
Special thanks to Lidia Morson Tramontozzi

12 11 10 9 8 7 6 5 4 3 2   8 9 10 11 12 13/0

Printed in the U.S.A.
First printing, April 2008

Dear Reader:

After several attempts to send us Ulysses Moore's fourth manuscript, Michael Merryweather finally succeeded. Reading it, you'll find that...well, you'll find out for yourself!

While we're extremely excited to tell you more about this mysterious adventure, we're also a little worried about our special correspondent. It seems he came very close to discovering where Kilmore Cove is hidden. Since that time, however, we haven't heard from him. Even his cell phone is shut off! As soon as we hear from him, we'll update you on his whereabouts. . . .

Your friends at Scholastic

From: Michael Merryweather
Date: February 3, 2006 4:24 PM
To: The editors at Scholastic Inc.
Subject: Kilmore Cove exists!

I've been trying every which way to get an e-mail out to you, but so far they all bounce back. Please let me know immediately if you get this. The manuscript is filled with so many surprises that it will absolutely leave you gasping. . . . Right now, though, I don't have time to say much more about it.

What's really bugging me is my failure to find Kilmore Cove, the phantom town. The day before yesterday I went looking for it. My only clue was the tourist guide of Kilmore Cove that a mysterious man (Ulysses Moore?) had left on my table at the outdoor cafe. I checked it out: The publishing house that printed it closed fifteen years ago and there don't seem to be any other copies in circulation.

I came to the suburbs of Kilmore Cove by car and traveled along the coast until I hit a detour. The roadblock had several DO NOT ENTER signs. So I got out of the car, moved the signs, and continued along the seacoast.

I should never have done that! At the very first curve, the asphalt road seemed to disintegrate. There were gigantic potholes all over the road. A distinguished-looking gentleman waved at me to stop and asked if I had missed the detour signs. Then I saw him signal to a man at the wheel of a backhoe, and I understood that it was time for us to turn back.

Once I returned to my bed-and-breakfast, I tried to send you the fourth manuscript before heading out again.

Talk to you soon, or at least I hope to. . . .

Michael

Contents

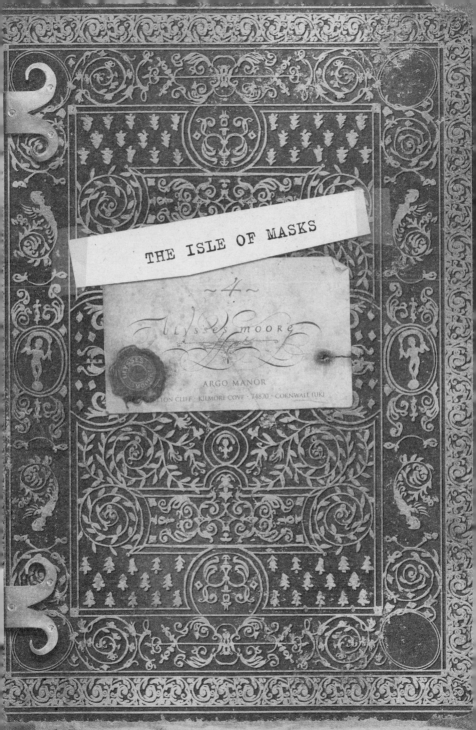

THE ISLE OF MASKS

~4~

Ulysses Moore

ARGO MANOR

SALTON CLIFF · KILMORE COVE · 74820 · CORNWALL (UK)

The lighthouse of Kilmore Cove suddenly lit up, stabbing the darkness with a sword of light. The beacon swept over the sea and the coastline, reaching beyond the dark waves, cutting slivers of light in the night sky. It passed over the town's roofs, stretching past the hills, sending frightened rabbits scurrying for safety.

When the light reached the ancient trees in Argo Manor's garden, it pushed past the blinds that covered the windows. In the attic, three people were bent over a battered old trunk that was covered with travel tags.

"It's only Leonard. . . ." said Nestor, the caretaker of the old house. He was keeping an eye on Jason and Julia while their parents moved their things from London.

"The lighthouse keeper," Julia explained for Jason's benefit.

Jason had not yet seen the lighthouse lit. He walked to the attic window and peered out into the night.

Jason and his twin sister, Julia, had had more adventures in the last two days than either had experienced in the previous eleven years of their lives. They had just moved from London to Kilmore Cove, a sleepy little town along the coast of

Cornwall. But there was nothing sleepy about what they'd discovered behind the mysterious door in the oldest room of their new home, Argo Manor. Its previous owner, Ulysses Moore, seemed to have left behind many secrets for the twins to discover. There was a long stone passageway full of riddles and puzzles that the kids had managed to decipher one by one. And the passageway led to something beyond the kids' wildest imaginations . . . a great sailing ship anchored in an enormous grotto. A sailing ship that could travel through time. The twins and their new friend, Rick Banner, had already journeyed to ancient Egypt.

Now the kids were planning their latest trip: to eighteenth-century Venice. They were on the trail of an inventor who'd disappeared years ago, taking with him the secret of the Doors to Time that existed all over Kilmore Cove. Jason, Julia, and Rick were determined to find him before Oblivia Newton, a sinister schemer who always seemed to be one step ahead of them, got to him.

"Awesome!" Jason murmured softly, as the light fell on him for a second time. His shadow lengthened until it reached the farthest recesses of the attic, onto the abandoned paintings and furniture covered with sheets. "Will it stay on all night?"

"Only if Leonard remembers," answered Nestor. "The light seems to come and go with no rhyme or reason."

Julia smiled to herself. For two nights Leonard had remembered to turn on the lighthouse beacon. The first night, the lighthouse — like a watchful eye — had kept her company while a storm raged and an intruder tried to break into Argo Manor.

Jason returned to Julia's side and knelt before the trunk. He helped his sister break the last of the locks and grasped the lid. A torn tag showed the words VENICE, ARTIFACTS, written in Ulysses Moore's distinctive handwriting.

"We've got it," said the boy, triumphant. He raised the lid. A cloud of dust puffed up. The lighthouse beacon moved across the ceiling.

"Beautiful," Julia murmured, lifting a soft red cloth out of the old trunk.

"It looks like a cape," ventured Jason. He gently inspected the cloth; its floral motif, red on red, revealed strange patterns, as if the material had been woven with silver threads. It was extremely worn and the hem was tattered.

The trunk contained three compartments, every one of which was marked with an old medallion and a white papier-mâché mask.

"Venetian masks!" exclaimed Julia. She carefully picked one up. The mask was a face with empty eyes, a pointed nose, and two golden tears. There were three masks resting on top of three black capes, all of which were clasped around the neck by two lacquered pins.

Under Nestor's watchful gaze, the twins arranged the items on the attic floor.

Inside the compartments, they found handkerchiefs with the initials U.M. and P.M., a pair of lace gloves, a long woolen scarf, a pin in the shape of a greyhound, theater glasses, a walking stick with a brass pommel, and an eighteenth-century map of Venice. The map was faded and fragile, scarcely legible. There were also comedy playbills and several invitations inside old envelopes on which were written SANTA ANGELO THEATER.

Jason and Julia studied every object, puzzling over its meaning. Nestor told them the little he knew about social life in old Venice from the stories that had been told to him by Ulysses Moore and his wife.

For almost an hour, instead of being in an old dusty attic among furniture covered with sheets, Jason and Julia imagined themselves in the magical city of Venice, surrounded by mysterious canals, cavernous ballrooms, masked wanderers, music, and laughter.

But slowly, surely, sleep dimmed their fantasies. Finally Nestor said, "I think it's time to get to bed. Tomorrow is a school day."

Jason placed a mask on his face. He turned and leered at his sister, thrusting the frightening mask toward her.

"Definitely an improvement," Julia noted, rolling her eyes.

A mist rose from the city's canals. It twisted and turned among the buildings, making them appear and disappear. The gondoliers rested inside the black hulls of their boats, woolen blankets pulled up tightly to their noses.

In Venice, only masked people came alive at night.

A figure wearing a skull mask walked stealthily along the canals of the old ghetto. The street signs, decayed by mold, had become scarce in this desolate part of the city. Yet the figure did not hesitate. She had an appointment to keep, one she could not miss. So she hurried along, intent on a single purpose.

After crossing a bridge that led to the eastern side of the city, she paused. She had come to a narrow opening between two old, battered buildings, with protruding gargoyles hanging above her head. The chimneys above were idle. The windows were dark.

This was it.

She had arrived at the Calle of the Dead.

"You are late," called a voice from the shadows.

It belonged to a man hidden behind a mask with a

black crow's beak. He wore a smoke-colored mantle that made him look like a mottled bird.

"I tried my best, but these blasted shoes!" the woman complained. She came to the steps that led to a narrow door and sat down. She rested for a few seconds before pulling off her impractical footwear. The woman stretched long, thin legs. She leaned her head back, revealing a long, slender neck.

"I can't breathe. . . ."

"Stop!" ordered the man with the bird's beak, guessing that the woman wanted to remove her mask. "I don't wish to know your identity."

"Very well," she replied. "We are here on business."

"Yes, of course," the man said. "I understand that you are looking for someone who has access to information. A finder, if you will. Well, I am that man. What do you want?"

"Not what, but who," she replied. "I'm looking for a man who is involved in the magical arts."

The man stepped closer, dragging his feet on the damp pavement. Fog rose from the canal and danced in the reflection of the moon. "I imagine you know the mandate of The Council of Ten regarding magic. In Venice, magic is forbidden. As are some books, gambling, and every shape and form of trickery, perceptual illusions, cardsharpers, swindlers, and charm vendors."

"That is why I need your help," she answered. "I know that The Council of Ten is responsible for all the dealings of a group of so-called secret guards of the city."

"You are well informed, madam," the man said. "I am proud to say that I am of that group. However, I do not even know the identity of the other secret guards. When we gather, we always wear masks — our true natures are never revealed. Tell me, then, for whom are you looking?"

"His name is Peter Dedalus."

The secret guard remained silent for a long time. "I am not familiar with that name," he said at last. "What is his business?"

"He is an inventor," she replied. "He builds machines, gadgets, and clocks."

"Clocks, did you say?"

"Clocks, yes," she said. "Clocks in every shape, style, and form."

"And what's so magical, or dangerous, about the behavior of this man?" he asked.

The woman pulled a bag from under her cloak. It was heavy with coins.

"Whoever helps me find Peter Dedalus will

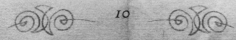

become very rich," she said. "Far richer than what a guard can ever make."

The man backed away. "This is bribery, corruption," he said. "A dangerous business indeed!"

The woman shrugged, still holding out the coin-filled bag. "Call it what you want. But if you assist me, you will be well rewarded."

And so it was agreed.

"Meet me tomorrow evening at six," said the man, "in the cafe at Saint Mark's Square."

The woman nodded. "And what shall I call you?"

"I answer to the name of Count Ashes," the man said.

"Very well, Count Ashes," the woman said. "We have a date. Tomorrow at six."

The man drifted, fading into the mist. Almost as an afterthought, he turned and asked, "And your name, madam?"

"Newton," answered the masked woman. "Like the English scientist. No relation, of course."

- Chapter 3 -
THE HEADMASTER

A loud bell echoed in the halls of the school, followed by shouts of joy in the classrooms.

A swarm of children raced down the stairs. Their shrieks were muffled only as they passed the headmaster's office, a door with yellow glass, behind which students imagined fearful consequences. Once they were beyond the office, when they felt safe under the great arch that looked toward the square, the happy noise resumed.

In the blink of an eye, Kilmore Cove's school had emptied.

Almost.

A boy who had gotten as far as the exit turned and hurried back toward the stairs. He took the steps two at a time and went into a classroom. He picked up the backpack that he had forgotten and moved to make his escape to the outside as quickly as he could. While passing the headmaster's office for the second time, a deep, powerful voice stopped him dead in his tracks.

"Stop!" thundered the headmaster. "Who might you be?"

"Jason Covenant, sir," answered the boy, turning on his heels.

Jason found himself facing a very tall man who was as skinny as a black crane. He had an austere demeanor.

"Covenant?" asked the headmaster. "I don't remember any Covenant in this school's student body."

"I'm sorry, Mr. . . . er, um . . ." Jason couldn't remember the name of the headmaster. "My sister and I came to town just a few days ago."

"Yes, of course! The Londoners!" the headmaster said. "The twins from Argo Manor!"

Jason nodded, eager to get away. But it seemed that the headmaster wished to talk.

"So tell me, young man. How do you like small town life?" he asked. "Kilmore Cove is nothing like London."

"I like it very much, sir," Jason answered.

"And how do you like living in such a . . . strange house?" the headmaster asked.

"Strange?" Jason repeated. "Why do you say that?"

The headmaster did not answer. Instead, he placed his hand on Jason's shoulder and guided him to the exit. The school yard was empty except for Julia and Rick. They could hear the laughter of faraway voices as the other children headed toward their homes. Julia and Rick looked at Jason anxiously, wondering what he'd gotten himself into now.

"I imagine this is your sister," said the headmaster.

"Oh no! That's Rick Banner," Jason answered,

intentionally misunderstanding the headmaster. "He lives down the street."

The headmaster said nothing.

"May I go now? Thank you, sir!" Jason said without waiting for an answer. He bolted toward his sister and his friend, grateful to escape.

"What did the old goat want?" Rick asked.

"I don't know," Jason said. "I think he wanted to ask me something. Too bad I couldn't even remember his name."

"Mr. Marriet," Rick said. "Mr. Ursus Marriet."

"Ursus?" repeated Julia. "Doesn't anybody in this town have a normal name?"

"My mother has a normal name," answered Rick.

"Yeah? What's that?"

"Mom."

"Har-har-har," Julia said in a slow drawl. "Great comedy, Rick. Wait till Hollywood finds out about you."

Jason interrupted their conversation. "He said that Argo Manor is a strange house."

"Oh?" Julia asked. "Strange in what way?"

"He didn't tell me," Jason said. "But his eyes were shining. You know, like he wanted to tell me something."

"Oh, don't pay any attention to Mr. Marriet," Rick scoffed. "We've got more important things to do."

"Oh yeah, right," Jason said. "Let's see. All we have to do today is travel through time to Venice, find Peter Dedalus before Oblivia Newton finds him, then try to discover the secret about how to control all the doors in town . . ."

". . . before Mom and Dad get home," added Julia. "Easy as pie."

They reached a wrought-iron streetlight on which two bicycles were chained. One was old and sturdy; the other was, to Jason's dismay, hot pink.

"I think we should all go our own ways," suggested Rick, pointing to a street that led to the train station. "I'll run home, grab my bike, and meet you at Argo Manor."

"Sounds good," Julia said. "I'll stop by the bookstore and ask about the guidebook to Kilmore Cove. I wish I grabbed it when I had the chance yesterday! Too bad Ms. Calypso caught me snooping."

Jason eyed the pink bicycle with disgust. "As for me, I'm going home before anybody sees me on top of this cotton-candy-colored heap of uncool."

"Yeah," deadpanned Julia, "you've got a reputation to protect."

"I'll see you soon," said Rick. He waved once, turned, and raced down the street.

CORNWALL GUIDE

KILMORE COVE

256
COLOR
PHOTOGRAPHS

TAVERNS AND PUBS | HISTORIC BUILDING | SHOPS AND MARKETS

DOUBLE McINNES EDITION LTD · Liverpool & South Seaside

The sign for Calypso's Island swayed in the gentle sea breeze. Julia pushed on the door, but it was locked.

"Oh great," she muttered. "Why is it closed in the middle of the day?"

Julia was eager to get her hands on *The Curious Traveler*, a slim guidebook to Kilmore Cove she had discovered in the store the previous day. Julia pondered the memo sheet covered with curious annotations that she had found inside the guide. Someone had noted that the town's railroad station ended nowhere, and that the statue in the center of town was of a king who had never existed. Two things that Nestor later confirmed were true.

Julia squished her face against the bookstore window. She had got the impression — more of a feeling, really — that someone on the other side of the glass was staring back at her.

"Ms. Calypso?" Julia called out apprehensively. She moved away and stood in the direct sunlight. The blue sky was dotted with puffs of clouds. From the church's steeple came the sound of slow, rhythmic bells.

Julia checked her watch. The bookstore should still be open. She tried again. And again, there was no answer.

"Of course!" Julia exclaimed, slapping her forehead. She crossed the square and went into the post office. Just as she had figured, Ms. Calypso was busy at her second job as a postal worker. She was seated behind a counter, wearing a green visor pulled down above her eyes.

"Ah, Julia," the woman said in greeting. "How may I help you today?"

"Actually, I had hoped to see you in the bookstore," Julia explained.

The small woman grimaced and pointed to several mail sacks. "I'm sorry, Julia. On Mondays, I'm on this side of the square."

The church bells sounded again. Ms. Calypso checked her watch, smiled, and rose from her chair. "Ah, the church bells have just announced the end to my job today as postal worker."

The woman came out from behind her desk and headed to the front door. "Do you need more books? Don't tell me that you've already finished the last one I gave you."

"Ah, well . . . um," stammered Julia, feeling guilty for not having read a single page of *Wuthering Heights*. "Actually, I haven't exactly — like, um, *totally* — totally finished it yet, but . . ."

"In that case," the diminutive bookseller asked

as they approached the bookstore, "how may I help you?"

"Do you remember when I came to make the phone call yesterday?" Julia asked.

Ms. Calypso smiled. "I am old, dear girl, but I haven't completely lost my marbles. Of course I remember — it was only yesterday." She inserted a thin, long key into the lock and turned it. The bell that announced all the store's comings and goings jingled merrily.

"Well, while I was calling, I, um, noticed a book that I was really interested in. . . ." Julia continued.

For a couple of seconds the two remained in the doorway. From inside, Julia heard a thump, as if a pile of books had fallen down.

Ms. Calypso made no sign of having heard it. Maybe she was getting senile after all.

"Could you tell me what the book was about?" Ms. Calypso asked. "You'll have to narrow it down a little if we hope to find it."

"It was called *The Curious Traveler*," Julia said. "It was an old guide to Kilmore Cove."

If a white fly wearing a purple tutu had flown in front of Ms. Calypso's eyes, she could not have been more dumbfounded. The expression on her face was one of total shock, but it lasted only a moment. Ms. Calypso recovered quickly, and the tiny woman once again wore a sweet, disarming smile.

"Oh, do you mean the red velvet pocketbook?" she asked.

"Yes, that's the one!"

"I am so sorry!" Ms. Calypso said, clasping her hands together. "It's been in the bookstore for at least twenty years, but I sold it to somebody last night, right after you left!"

It was Julia's turn to be surprised. "Sold it?"

"Yes, to a man who was passing through town. A tourist, you know. He told me, 'There's really very little of interest around here.' As you can imagine, I replied, 'Take a boat tour around the bay . . . and bring along a good book!'"

Ms. Calypso laughed. "But oh, he was terribly insistent. Most persuasive, he was. So I remembered that old guide, *The Curious Traveler*, and dug it up. I told him that it was very old and out of date, but he didn't seem to care. He bought it right off. A strange bird, I'll say that much."

"Can you describe him?" Julia asked.

"He was an elegant-looking gentleman, I must say," answered Ms. Calypso, blushing slightly. "Tall, well dressed, distinguished. Well educated, I should think," she added. "An Oxford type, I suspect."

Julia felt a wave of panic in her chest. Could it possibly be a coincidence that someone else wanted this book that had been sitting on the shelf for over twenty years? Who was this man? And why now? Julia absently felt in her pocket for the four keys to the Door to Time. They suddenly felt very heavy, like a burden she carried.

"We could try ordering another copy if it's still in print," Ms. Calypso said. But when she turned to look at Julia, Ms. Calypso realized that the girl had vanished. Gone, without even saying good-bye.

"Londoners are a strange lot," Ms. Calypso noted.

Rick Banner made a beeline for home. He went upstairs, greeted his mother, grabbed a snack, gobbled it down while standing over the kitchen counter, and dashed out the door, bounding down the stairs three steps at a time. Rick got to the street, looked up, and met his mother's gaze looking out the window. She waved to him, a slight gesture with her hand. Rick waved back, smiled brightly, and headed toward the church.

St. Jacob's was a tall, narrow building. Rick stood outside and stared at it, uncertain about his next move. In the rarefied silence of the church surroundings, it felt as if thousands of sharp nettles were forcing him to think about things that he preferred to keep buried. Rick squelched the memory of his father's funeral, took a deep breath, and opened the door.

"Oh, bless you, just in time!" exclaimed Father Phoenix, the parish pastor. He held a long mop in his hands. "You came to help me, Rick Banner, didn't you?" As always, Father Phoenix was direct and jovial. "Would you please assist me with this pail?"

The pail in question was filled with soapy water. Rick and the priest dragged the heavy pail outside. Father Phoenix explained that the front of the church desperately needed cleaning.

"I've been meaning to give it a good wash for months," the priest said, plunging the mop into the water and scrubbing it against the facade of the church.

Rick watched the priest with admiration. Father Phoenix was one of those people who made do with whatever they had without complaint. The gentle priest always found time for everyone.

"What's on your mind, Rick?" he prompted, while swishing the mop against the church walls. "Don't worry, it's just you and me. No one else is around."

Rick looked about him and hesitated. He drew close to the priest and said, "It's about Mr. Moore."

Father Phoenix put down the mop and gave Rick his full attention. "Ulysses Moore? What does Mr. Moore have to do with you?"

Rick told him about his new friends at Argo Manor. The priest listened while Rick described his new friends. Father Phoenix was glad the town had gotten new residents. But he was surprised by Rick's final question.

"You want to know about the funeral?" the priest asked.

"Yes," Rick answered. It was an idea that Rick couldn't shake. He kept asking himself, "What if?" What if Jason was right? What if Ulysses Moore hadn't really died? He wondered why neither of the Moores had been buried in Kilmore Cove's cemetery.

Rick confided his doubts to Father Phoenix, who listened quietly and attentively.

"I wasn't in town when it happened," the priest

explained after Rick had finished. "I was away on church business."

"I see," Rick said. "Do you know why he isn't buried in the town cemetery?"

"The explanation is simple, Rick," the priest explained. "The Moores are private people, in death as in life. They have their own family mausoleum on top of the hill at Argo Manor."

"A mausoleum? What's a mausoleum?" Rick wondered.

"A private tomb, I guess you could call it," the priest explained. "The Moores' mausoleum is at the entrance of Turtle Park. That's why not a single Moore from past generations is buried in Kilmore Cove's cemetery."

Rick quickly rattled off a dozen questions, which the priest waved away, laughing. "Don't ask an old man numbers and dates, dear boy," joked Father Phoenix. "I can scarcely remember what I had for breakfast."

"Who should I ask?" Rick inquired.

"Fred Naptime," answered Father Phoenix.

Rick knew all about Fred Naptime, who was something of a local legend. He earned his nickname — Naptime was not, of course, his real name — because townsfolk said he spent the entire day half-asleep, dreamily turning the pages of his newspaper. Rick had never actually spoken to the man. He asked how he might contact Mr. Naptime.

"See that building on the opposite side of the square?" the priest said, pointing to a squat brick building. "There's a small door to the left leading to what I call 'The Paper Office.' It's actually the archives of all the births and deaths of the residents of this town. Deeds, marriage certificates, all manner of legal documents are kept there."

"Is it okay for me to go there?" Rick asked.

"It's Fred's job to take care of all the records and permits of the county," Father Phoenix responded. "Tell him that you wish to see the records that pertain to Ulysses Moore. If Fred gives you a hard time, just tell him you're doing a favor for me."

Rick thanked the priest for his kindness and set off eagerly for his meeting with the famous Fred Naptime.

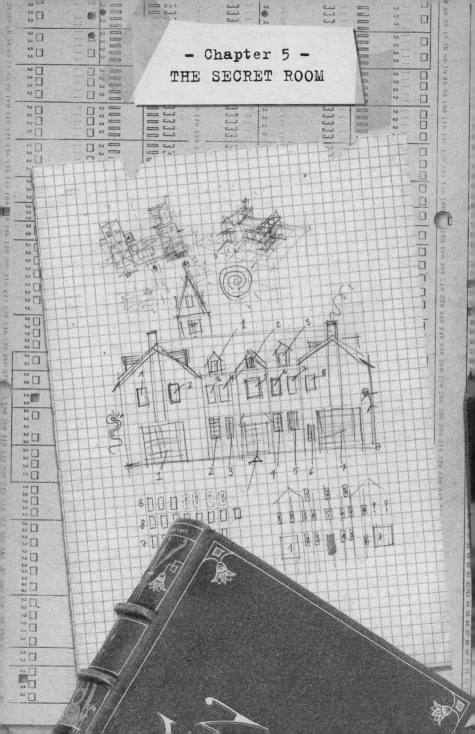

J ason sat outside Argo Manor reading intently from a book titled *A Guide to Paranormal Creatures*.

According to the book, ghosts preferred to haunt old houses that often contain secret rooms. One way to find out whether or not an old house had a secret room was to count the number of windows visible from the outside.

With his back resting against the old sycamore tree, Jason took a sheet of graph paper, placed it on the back of the manual, and began counting the windows on the ground floor. Seven. Then he counted those on the second floor. Eight.

Nestor stuck his head out of the kitchen door. "Jason! Teatime."

"I'm coming!" answered the boy. He rose to his feet, staring at the great old manor. Jason whispered, "If you are hiding in a secret room, Ulysses Moore, I won't rest until I find you. . . ."

The kitchen table had been set for three. But so far, there was no sign of Julia and Rick.

"If it gets cold, too bad for them," grumbled Nestor.

The kids had begun the preparations for their next incredible journey: three Venetian capes, three flashlights, a knapsack, a couple of yards of rope, a camera, a Swiss army knife, a compass, the map of eighteenth-century Venice, and Ulysses Moore's old journal. Nestor was about to pick up the journal when the phone rang.

"No, Mrs. Covenant," Nestor said into the phone, signaling to Jason to remain quiet. "Yes, of course, they went to school! No problems at all. Yes. Of course. Of course I'll tell them: You may arrive tonight, or at the latest, tomorrow morning. I'm so sorry you're having so much trouble with the move . . . few people know how to do their jobs right nowadays. Don't worry. Try again later. Yes, a little later. Good luck."

A man came out of the shadows from behind the bookshelves. "I'm sorry about the noise," he apologized. "Do you think she suspected anything?"

"Oh, don't worry," answered Ms. Calypso. "She didn't notice a thing."

The man sighed deeply. "How did she seem to you? Calm?"

The corners of Ms. Calypso's mouth turned downward. "I may have frightened her a little," she admitted. "I told her everything that you said, even if I don't agree with this sort of deception. She's just a child."

"I'm sorry, but it was necessary," the man said. "I don't want to take her attention away from the matter at hand. We can't have any distractions, not now, not when we are so close. . . ."

"You may be right," said the bookstore owner. "But I think she is even more curious than before."

The man took a book from his pocket, titled *The Curious Traveler.* "There was a sheet of paper inside the guide," he said, with some alarm in his voice. "Where is it?"

"Julia might have taken it yesterday when she discovered the book," Ms. Calypso answered.

The man frowned, unhappy over this turn of events.

"She won't understand your scribbled notes," Ms. Calypso reassured him. "Or were the notes written by your friend?"

"No names, please."

"Why not?" the woman protested. "Are you afraid someone is eavesdropping?"

"Perhaps," the man answered. "Remember, we have enemies." He stared out the window. "Do you think she's really gone?"

Ms. Calypso nodded. She went to the back of the bookstore, looked outside, and said, "I see her. Julia is pedaling up the cliffside road, on her way back to Argo Manor."

"That cliff is dangerous," whispered the man. He stuffed the guide into his pocket. With a nod of his head he said, "Time for me to weigh anchor."

"And go so soon?" Ms. Calypso said in surprise. "Where are you off to in such a hurry?"

"You are a snoopy woman, Calypso," the man said with a grin.

"Yes, I am!" she retorted. "That's because you never tell me anything!"

When she returned from the back window, Calypso realized that she was alone.

The man was gone.

The bell on the door had made no sound.

"I couldn't find a window to a secret room," Jason announced, ladling stew into his dish. "But that doesn't mean that there isn't one. . . ."

Jason leafed through the pages of his book. He read out loud: "*A secret room may also be walled in without windows. To discover a secret walled room, you need to measure the area of the house from the outside, and then that of every room inside the house. By simply subtracting the . . .*"

"Jason," interrupted Nestor, "I've been here for years. There aren't any other secret rooms in this house."

"Other?" Jason asked.

"Other than the one before the Door to Time."

"That's the point," noted Jason. "The round room that's at the other side of the Door to Time has four exits. One leads to Argo Manor, the second leads to the cave where the *Metis* is docked. But where do the other two go?"

Nestor shrugged. Apparently uninterested, he went back to washing dishes.

"See, there could be secret rooms dug under Argo Manor all over the place," Jason continued. "You know, like those places where the ancient Romans buried their dead. You know what I mean. What are they called? Kit, cat . . . I got it! Catacombs! After all, isn't this an ancient Roman house?"

"Well, yes," Nestor answered. "There was once an ancient watchtower on this cliff."

"Therefore, my hypothesis could be correct!" Jason exclaimed. "Maybe Ulysses Moore's secret room is in one of those tunnels. Maybe, just maybe, that's where he is hiding. From time to time he comes out of the Door to Time here and leaves us the clues we need. . . . That's it! That's it, exactly!" Jason said. "Ulysses Moore is helping us. But why?"

"Oh, Jason," Nestor said. "You are filled with too many absurd ideas. You've got to come to your senses."

Jason didn't believe everything that Nestor had told him about Ulysses Moore and Kilmore Cove. It was as if he was hiding something. Jason could not shake the sensation of being watched. And he was convinced he was following clues that were left by Ulysses himself.

"What if he isn't dead," Jason offered, trying a new tactic, "but he's a prisoner somewhere?"

"Jason, please," Nestor said. "You'll make my head explode. Today you need to find Peter Dedalus. It's almost certain that Oblivia Newton is searching for that key."

"Right," Jason agreed.

Julia suddenly raced into the kitchen, winded from the long bicycle ride. She announced, "It disappeared! Gone! It isn't there anymore!"

"What's gone?" asked Nestor.

"The tourist guide to Kilmore Cove!" Julia replied as she dumped her backpack on the floor and sat at the table.

Julia told them about what happened at the bookstore.

"It can't be a coincidence," Jason said. "Someone is bent on stopping us from finding out the truth about Kilmore Cove."

"Who do you think it could be?" Julia asked.

"It doesn't sound like the work of Oblivia Newton. . . ." murmured Nestor.

The kids looked at him, puzzled.

"Ms. Calypso told you it was a man who bought the guide," Nestor said. "A stranger, correct?"

Julia nodded in agreement.

"Did Ms. Calypso look frightened?" Nestor asked.

Julia shook her head. "No, she seemed calm, normal. I was the one who got jumpy."

She tried to describe the strange shiver she felt when she looked into the shop. It felt as if someone was lurking inside the bookstore.

"What did he look like?" Jason asked.

"I didn't say there definitely was somebody in the bookstore," Julia pointed out. "I said that it was *as if* someone was in it."

"Like a ghost?" offered Jason.

"Oh no! Here we go again!" Nestor exclaimed.

"It's not that crazy," Jason insisted. "Last night

the ghost told us to go to Venice — and he did it by banging on the tower window. . . ."

Julia remembered. She had heard a noise, went up to see what it was, and found a model of a gondola and a notebook on the desk. It was as if they had been left for them, like a clue, or an arrow pointing them in the right direction.

The notebook contained the details of a trip to eighteenth-century Venice, 1751 to be exact. The journal was written in Ulysses Moore's distinctive hand.

WARNING - DANGER

MOVING MACHINERY

AUTHORIZED PERSONNEL ONLY

The door opened on a long, sloping hall, at the end of which the pale glow of a lamp glimmered. The door clicked shut behind the boy automatically. Rick walked cautiously, looking this way and that, until he heard a voice. "This way, please."

Rick approached a man seated on a stool before an enormous fan. He had a newspaper neatly folded on his lap. The room was cluttered and dank. His desk was littered with scattered sheets of paper. The walls were covered with old paintings. A massive filing cabinet sat in the corner. A pair of worn-out leather chairs completed the room.

A bronze sign above a door read:

ARCHIVES

AUTHORIZED PERSONNEL ONLY

"May I help you?" asked the man. He wore a pair of gray woolen pants that reached to his ankles, and a red flannel shirt. The air from the fan made his long sideburns vibrate. Rick introduced himself and quickly explained his request.

"Yes, by Jove! We are here to serve, and serve we will. Please sign this sheet," Fred Naptime instructed.

The table was so tall that Rick had to stand on his tiptoes to sign the visitor's log.

"What exactly do you want to know about the Moore family?" asked the clerk. As Rick explained what he was looking for, the man opened several drawers of the filing cabinet and, after some time searching, took out about a dozen perforated index cards. He studied them, turned them over, and stared at them against the light.

"Perfect. Indeed, yes. These should be correct."

Fred Naptime disappeared behind the archive door. Rick heard him whistling. Soon the whistle was drowned by the clatter of what sounded like a large typewriter, followed by rattling sounds similar to those of a massive garbage truck. As the minutes passed, Fred's whistles turned into a kind of laborious gasping.

Curious, Rick peeked through the archive door, which had been left ajar. The room was entirely filled by an enormous metal machine, featuring levers and buttons of every size and description, tubes, and flashing lights. Fred Naptime was sliding the index cards into an opening that sucked them up in a gulp.

The machine spit out several sheets of paper. "By Jove!" mumbled the old clerk. Rick deftly stepped away from the door as Fred Naptime returned.

"Got it!" he said happily, waving the sheets in front of the fan so they could dry.

"Remarkable, isn't it?" he continued. "In a few minutes the Old Owl spewed out the pertinent information." He returned the punched cards to the filing cabinet and handed Rick the result of his work.

"And they dare call me Naptime. . . ." he said, eyes twinkling with satisfaction.

Rick gave a cursory look at what he held in his hands: a long list of all the ancestors of the Moore family, dating back several centuries. He scanned down to the two names that interested him the most.

```
Kilmore Cove's City Hall
Births, Marriages, Deaths, and Residences
Moore, Ulysses — born in Edinburgh,
   Scotland.

Age 63. Married to Penelope Sauri.
   Presumably deceased (accidental fall
   from Salton Cliff).
Moore, Sauri, Penelope — born in Venice,
```

Italy. Age 57. Married to Ulysses Moore.
Presumably deceased (accidental fall
from Salton Cliff).

Official Status: Awaiting official
  declaration of death
Heirs or relatives to the sixth degree:
  None
Executor: Nestor MacDouglas

Fred Naptime peeked over Rick's shoulder. "That's one treacherous cliff, eh?" he remarked. He pointed a long, bony finger to the words "awaiting official declaration of death."

"It's the law," he explained. "When the body is not recovered, at least ten years need to pass from the day of disappearance before that person can be declared officially dead."

"Their bodies were never recovered?" Rick asked.

"The sea, she swallowed them whole," Fred Naptime answered. "And she never coughed them back up."

"So . . . legally," Rick concluded, "Mr. and Mrs. Moore are not dead."

"Yes, *legally*," Fred replied, placing emphasis on

that technicality. "Let it suffice to say that our records are meticulous, but . . . Salton Cliff climbs to unforgiving heights. The sea swept them away . . . and the fish probably feasted that night. A sad end, indeed."

Rick suddenly thought of his father, lost at sea, and of the sea's strong currents, and of Manfred, Oblivia Newton's henchman, who had fallen from the same cliff.

But Manfred had survived.

It was possible to fall . . . and still live.

Fred Naptime added, "That machine, the Old Owl, never makes mistakes. In the thirty years I've worked here, it has functioned perfectly. Never broke down, not even for a day. Peculiar, isn't it? You'd think a machine would break every once in a while. But not the Old Owl. It has one flaw only: the way it types the *d*, obviously. Do you see how it is raised higher than the other letters? What I believe is," he said in a conspiratorial whisper, "is that it's not a mistake at all. Nope, it's the Old Owl's fingerprint."

"What do you mean?" Rick asked.

"The Old Owl is the last, great machine made by Dedalus before he . . . disappeared."

"Dedalus?" Rick echoed.

"Yes, don't you remember the clockmaker who vanished a couple of years ago?" the old man asked.

Rick was momentarily speechless. "Do you mean to say that machine in there, the one that controls the archives for all of Kilmore Cove, was built by Peter Dedalus?"

"I didn't *mean* to say it," Fred Naptime retorted. "I believe I just *did* say it. Yes, yes, of course. The Old Owl! It unravels all the paper, pamphlets, and booklets in the archives and finds all the records without losing a sheet. Not a single sheet! It's a mechanical wonder. What's more, it's also an old-fashioned printing press. That Dedalus, he was a clever one, indeed. The Owl is only gears and springs, yet it doesn't miss a beat. It works even in the dark, without electricity!"

Rick looked at the sheets with a kind of reverential respect. He asked, "If you don't mind, may I please make a second search?'

The sound of St. Jacob's bells chimed in the distance.

"Hmm . . . technically, as of this moment the office is closed. But I could make an exception," Fred Naptime said. "What are you looking for?"

"Peter Dedalus," answered Rick.

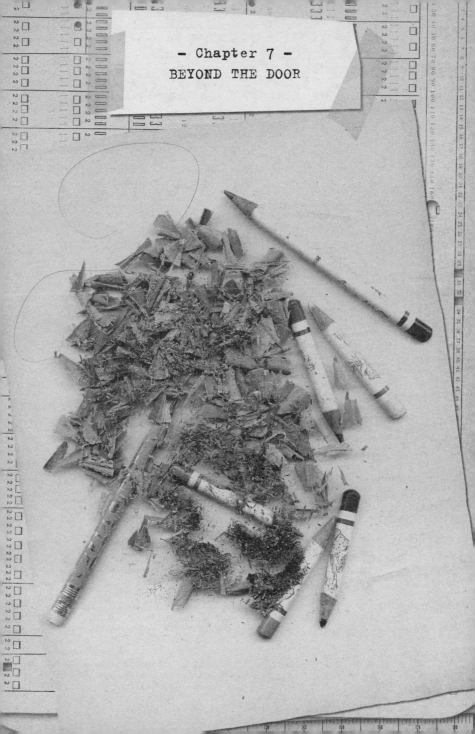

"Is this really necessary?" Julia asked Jason.

"I'm almost finished," Jason replied. He returned his attention to his book, reading the instructions with care.

Half intrigued, half exasperated, Julia denied the impulse to read over her brother's shoulder. *Did that book of his* really *advise readers to rub the doors of the house with egg whites? Was Jason really going to sprinkle flour in the halls?* It was insane.

"All these tricks aren't going to scare away any ghosts," she scoffed. "However, you do have the makings of a delicious crumb cake."

"Har-har," Jason muttered.

"Mom will freak," Julia added.

Jason shook his head. "Nope, she'll never see it. I'll remove the traps before she even returns."

"Traps?" Julia echoed, incredulously. "Really, Jason. I think you've flipped your lid this time."

Jason finished brushing the egg whites on the bathroom door. Suddenly, he turned to Julia and plucked out a strand of her hair.

"Ouch! What are you doing?"

"I needed a long hair," he explained, as if it wasn't already obvious enough. He placed Julia's hair on the door molding until it stuck to the egg whites. Jason smiled with satisfaction and announced, "The perfect ghost-catcher!"

Julia stepped toward the bathroom.

"Stop! Don't move!" he advised. Jason gestured to a thin layer of flour on the floor, which, according to the *Guide to Paranormal Creatures*, would serve to get "footprints" of the ghost.

"Since when do ghosts have feet?" Julia groaned. "What do they wear, high-tops?"

Her brother made her crazy sometimes, even if he was her twin. She decided to wait for Rick downstairs. Once he showed up, they'd be on their way . . . to Venice, in the year 1751!

Rick pulled up on his bicycle, his breath unlabored even after the arduous climb up the long, winding cliff road.

"Everything okay?" he asked.

Julia smiled and tilted her head in the direction of the house. "Jason is upstairs setting traps for ghosts," she replied. "He seems to think there's a ghost roaming the house."

"I see," Rick said.

"Yes," Julia answered, smiling widely now. "Either Ulysses Moore, or Penelope Moore, or, I suppose, Casper the Friendly."

Rick laughed — Julia's dry wit and deadpan

delivery always made him laugh. He really enjoyed her company.

They walked together to the terrace, passing in front of the statue of the fisherwoman intent on mending her broken net. A pleasant warmth filtered through the picture windows. For a moment Julia had the urge to race down to the beach with Rick — forget all about secret doors and missing keys — just the two of them swimming in the swirling water, laughing.

"I wonder what the weather is like today in Venice," Rick said, grinning.

"We'll find out soon enough," Julia said brightly. She put aside her foolish thoughts and led Rick into the kitchen, where Nestor waited.

"Hello, Nestor," Rick said. "I learned an interesting fact about you today."

Nestor raised an eyebrow.

"Yes, I discovered that your last name is MacDouglas," Rick said.

"Fascinating," Nestor replied dryly. The old caretaker went to the sink, filled a watering can, and stepped outside to the garden.

"He's grumpy," Rick noted.

"I don't think he's exactly thrilled with Jason," Julia replied. "After all, my brother is gluing hair to trap ghosts, sprinkling graphite dust on the mirrors, and . . ."

"Gluing hair?" Rick echoed, laughing.

Julia shrugged. "He's, like, sooooo weird."

Rick was curious nonetheless. "Why graphite?"

"According to Jason's book, if a ghost looks in a mirror that was dusted with graphite, he'll leave his image on the mirror. So he ground all the graphite in the pencils he found in the house and dusted it on the mirrored door of Ulysses Moore's office," she explained.

"Speaking of Ulysses Moore," Rick said, "I learned some very interesting things in town today." He showed Julia the papers he'd retrieved from Fred Naptime. Quickly, he filled her in on his trip to the archive office.

"This is a list of his ancestors," Rick explained, handing a sheet of paper to Julia. "We should probably compare it to the portraits hanging on the staircase wall. This next page, though, is the one that's really strange. It's what we got from our search on Peter Dedalus."

She stared at the paper, perplexed. "What does it mean?" she asked.

"I asked the same question," Rick replied.

The sheet read:

(COUNT OF ITEM OF TRACER (1) = 0
1 2 3 4 5 6 7 8 9 10 11 12 13 14 15 16 17 18 19 20 21 22 23 24 25 26 27 28 29 30 31 32 33 34 35 36 37 38 39 40

```
    This  machine  is  not  authorized  to
release information regarding the person
you are researching. If you wish to chal-
lenge it, you may do so, provided you use
the correct key and write DEDA. To avoid
further disappointments, please note that
the right key is not below.
```

Rick said, "We tried some alternate searches, like inputting DEDA instead of DEDALUS, but nothing worked."

Chewing on her lower lip, Julia stared at the printed page for a long while. "Beats the heck out of me," she admitted. "*Please note that the right key is not below?* I mean, what does *that* mean?"

Jason finally joined them downstairs. Rick told the twins about the Moores' private mausoleum, the family tomb on top of the hill in Turtle Park where all the Moores were buried.

"Supposedly," Jason said.

"Yes," Rick agreed. "I'm getting to the point where I don't believe anything unless I see it for myself."

"There's no time for that now," Julia interrupted. "The mission to Venice is more urgent."

The three adventurers gathered their equipment

for the trip. Everything they needed — or thought they needed — was prepared.

Nestor reentered the house and set his watering can on the granite countertop. He watched gravely as Julia checked her pockets for the four keys to the mysterious doors. She met his gaze, took a deep breath, and said, "Let's rock and roll."

Click, click, click, click.

The four keys turned the locks of the Door to Time.

The great door opened.

Beyond the threshold . . . infinite mystery.

They paused, hesitating.

Jason took the first step. His flashlight illuminated the passageway that led to a circular room. Rick followed, hauling a pack on his back. Julia, entering last, felt a wave of foreboding. A sense that great danger awaited them. She turned to look at Nestor.

He watched her, grim-faced. "Be careful," the old man said. "Take no unnecessary risks. Promise me!"

Julia nodded, the words caught in her throat.

"If you don't find Peter, if there's any trouble whatsoever, then come right home," Nestor called, peering after them.

In the round room, Jason paused. He studied each of the four archways, hoping to find some kind of a clue. One archway led back to Argo Manor, another led below. The other two, as the rhyme in the parchment that had led them here had foretold, led to death.

The flashlight revealed animal figures that had been carved above the doors to each stone archway. One had fish, another bulls, a third featured fireflies, and the last — the path that led back to Argo Manor — albatrosses.

Albatrosses, Jason thought: *a cross to bear, a burden to share.*

"*Of four, two mean death on the spot, and one of the four will lead below,*" Jason recited, his voice scarcely above a whisper.

From Argo Manor, Nestor called out one last bit of advice. "Music! Remember that Peter was an ardent lover of music!"

And with those words, the Door to Time slammed shut.

Julia, Jason, and Rick walked with determined steps. They didn't chat or joke; their stride was purposeful, their mood serious.

At last they came to the grotto's second landing. Each remembered what had happened in this same spot just two days earlier, when persistent drafts made the candle gutter and fade. They had feared they might be trapped in the darkness forever.

Of four, two mean death. . . .

But this time, they had a flashlight. The three explorers descended the wet, slippery stairs, crawling beneath large stones that had collapsed and blocked part of the passageway. They passed over the pit in which Jason had let the earth-lights fall. They entered the room with the perilous chute. Thinking back to what happened the last time, Rick asked, "Did we bring it?"

"Right here!" Julia said, showing him the *Dictionary of Forgotten Languages*. She walked to the opening of the chute and, as she had been before, was the first to slide down. Jason and Rick followed close behind, shouting as they fell.

They had reached the subterranean grotto.

During the day, without the thousand fireflies to give it light, the grotto looked different. Arrows of light shot from the ceiling, drawing bright circles on the beach. The shafts of light gave the hallucinatory impression that the cave was filled with columns that held up the great vault of the grotto. The rock walls curved above them like an inverted bowl.

"It's beautiful. Like a forest of light," Julia whispered.

The *Metis* had returned from the other side of the interior cove and now rested peacefully at the wooden pier. The graceful vessel beckoned in the water, like an elegant invitation to distant adventures. The ropes still dangled from the mainmast. The oars were in the same place where Rick and Julia had left them.

Julia brushed her hand over the Greek letters of the ship's name. "Are we ready to do this?" she asked, a touch of apprehension in her voice.

In answer, the boys immediately hoisted their gear on deck, bounded onto the ship, and headed directly to the cabin.

Lying on top of the table was a black, leatherbound journal, the captain's log. Jason took a pen from his backpack and confidently opened the book to the first blank page. In bold letters he wrote: "*I, Jason Covenant, accompanied by my sister, Julia,* and my friend Rick Banner, am once again captain of the Metis. *It is time again for us to travel across the waters . . . and back in time!"*

The anchor raised, the *Metis* drifted from the pier. On the far side of the mirror-like water, Rick glimpsed the closed door with its massive stone archway.

"Jason, what are we supposed to do now?" asked his sister. "Should we use the oars?"

"Steady," whispered the young captain. He opened Ulysses Moore's journal and read: "*. . . like the rest of the city's buildings, it is built on top of oak pilings dug deep into the mud. In the market square, there is a hunchback who is said to bring good luck. Gondolas can be viewed gliding along the Grand Canal. Ladies take their walks in elegant, long dresses, their waists constricted by whalebone corsets.*"

Jason closed the book, placed his hand on the helm, and cried, "To Venice, Eighteenth Century!"

The captain closed his eyes.

When he opened them again, a gust of wind blasted against the ship. The *Metis* jerked forward, pointing its bow toward the far shore.

"Jason!" Julia yelled to her brother. "Are you doing this?"

The sea surged as the wind picked up velocity, sending heavy sprays of water onto the deck. The camera fell overboard and disappeared into the sea.

"Jason!" Julia desperately called.

But it was as if he could not hear. Jason was mesmerized by the psychedelic patterns of light and swirling water that filled the cave like a painter's abstract canvas. The columns of light became fluid, the seawater turned to foggy mist, and the wind blew mercilessly against the ship. The bow of the *Metis* heaved into the sea.

"Onward!" Jason cried, like a boy possessed, a visionary at the heart of a journey, screaming to the sea itself. "Onward! Onward!" Jason saw a sea that was infinite, a sea where clouds thickened and gathered. A sun rose and set simultaneously, with ever-changing colors. He saw a world populated by enigmatic creatures searching unfathomable mysteries, and a sea that spanned from the dawn of time to final dusk.

A sea that sang.

Jason gripped the rudder and understood that he was part of that song.

Everything was connected! Every — living — thing! His soul rocketed into space.

Jason understood that the song had connected them all, that he was riding that song like a wave onto the shore of infinite possibility. He saw magical ships intersecting his route. The ships had exotic travelers standing on their bridges and smiling, waving to him.

Then the ships he saw, or thought he saw, slipped away like silvery gliding fish.

When he opened his eyes, they had arrived at the far shore. At a different place in time.

Led by Jason, the three travelers disembarked from the *Metis* and climbed stairs that led to a lone door with an archway decorated by three turtles. As they had done before on their trip to ancient Egypt, they pushed the door open. But this time they found themselves on the threshold of a quiet stone courtyard. A gallery of small arches surrounded a hexagonal well in the center.

"Do you think we're in Venice?" Julia asked.

"I think so," whispered Rick, not wishing to draw attention to himself.

Sheltered by the Door to Time, the kids stayed immobile a few seconds, waiting to see if there was anyone in the courtyard. Then they took a few, cautious steps toward the well.

As they got used to their new surroundings, Jason, Rick, and Julia became aware of the different sounds and smells. They heard the distant sound of voices and the rhythmic lapping of water. They went up a stairway and entered the gallery on the second floor. From there, they could see an expanse of roofs that stopped where the sea began.

The house where they stood gave the appearance of having been unoccupied for many years. Julia went to a window at the end of the gallery. She let out a muffled gasp, for what she saw overwhelmed

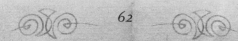

her emotions. She faced a grand canal filled with wooden boats with colorful, billowing sails. Lines of rowers, thick-muscled men, lowered and raised their wooden handles in formation, plunging the oars into the water. On a green island on the other side of the canal, cupolas and steeples shined in the sun. Directly beneath the window she saw a long, white stone embankment extending in both directions. It was crowded with people walking briskly to and fro. A short distance away, two beggars were making their dog dance to the sound of their flute.

Rick joined Julia, pressing against her, shoulder to shoulder, amazed at the scene before them.

"What a sight!" Rick murmured.

"I'm speechless," Julia said.

"That's a first," Rick noted with a sly grin.

Jason smiled happily. He had been able to captain the *Metis* exactly where he had planned. It was as if the ship answered to the beck and call of his own heart.

The kids put on their Venetian capes and went down into the courtyard. They raised the iron bars that closed the massive door from the inside and stepped out. In spite of the sun, the air was cool. They glanced back. Seen from the outside, the house did not seem abandoned. An old, tattered English flag was nailed on the door.

"*Cabot House, explorers . . .*" Jason read from Ulysses Moore's journal. "*John and his son Sebastian sailed for the king of England in search of a route to China. . . .*"

"That explains the English flag," Rick commented.

"*The two discovered the Island of Newfoundland and Canada. All traces of John were lost during an expedition to the Labrador Peninsula. Nobody knows where he disappeared. . . .*"

"Typical Ulysses," Julia said, "everything shrouded in mystery. Nothing is easy with that guy."

Jason continued reading. "The journal claims that people began to think that the Cabot family was cursed."

"Hmmmm. That might explain why this house has been left abandoned," Rick reasoned.

The street was bustling with activity. Men carried large wicker baskets filled with fish, fruit, and spices. Merchants sold chickens and singing birds. Men and women walked around in masks like the ones in Ulysses Moore's attic. Others promenaded stiffly, like brooms, showing off expensive clothes of the finest lace and embroidery.

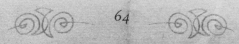

Jason spread out a map on the white cobblestones. He tried to figure out where they were in the city. They found Cabot House along Caste Rio, a short distance from the Arsenal, the shipbuilding quarter. To their immediate right was the main piazza of the city, Saint Mark's Square. On their left was the berth of Venice, the gateway to the sea.

"How do we begin to search this vast city for a single clockmaker?" Rick wondered. The task suddenly seemed hopeless.

"Typical male," Julia chided, "always afraid to ask directions." She pointed at the two beggars they had spied from the window.

"What are you going to do? Ask where Peter Dedalus lives?" snapped Jason.

"Watch and learn, brother," Julia said confidently. "Watch and learn." She grabbed Rick by the arm and led him toward the teenage street urchins.

"Hey!" Rick exclaimed. "I just noticed that my watch still works!"

"How could that be?" Julia wondered. "Mine stopped, just like the last time when we sailed on the *Metis.*"

Rick shrugged. "Well, I guess Peter's watches are made to travel in time!"

The beggar girl, dressed in dirty rags, stepped

toward Rick. "Oh, it's very pretty!" she enthused, admiring Rick's sparkling watch.

Her partner, a tall, sinewy, scraggly-haired boy, crowded close to Rick. "Yes, very valuable," he purred greedily.

Rick instinctively stepped back, burying his watch in his front pocket. The two street urchins gave him an uneasy feeling. He cast a look at Julia, trying to signal her: *Let's get away from these two.*

If Julia noticed Rick's apprehension, she ignored it. With a sunny smile, she said, "Can we please ask you something?"

The street boy answered with an exaggerated bow. "At your service!"

Julia smiled. "We're looking for . . . a clockmaker."

The boy looked questioningly at his friend. They didn't understand.

"A clockmaker," Julia repeated. "Um, let's see, a person who makes clocks or watches, like his watch," she said, gesturing to Rick. "You know, um, *tick-tock*?"

"Ah, yes, *tick-tock*," the boy replied, nodding enthusiastically. "Machines for the time."

"Where can we find them?" Julia asked. "Are they sold at the market? Are there shops?"

"Come, come with me," the beggar said, smiling, eyes full of mischief.

Rick placed his hand on Julia's elbow. He shook his head warily.

The beggar saw this and stepped back, smiling brightly. He placed two hands on his chest, then held them out, open-palmed. "Please, it is my honor. You can trust me."

Their dog, a dirty puppy with matted fur, began to sniff around Rick. He smiled at it, but didn't get too close — the mutt had obviously not been washed in months.

The scraggly-haired urchin turned to his female companion. "Listen, Esme! Our new friends seek a clockmaker. Do you understand?"

The girl gazed at him in puzzlement. Her face was covered in ashes and dirt.

Finally, the boy pointed down the street. "Go straight, my friends," he explained. "You will come to the Plaza de San Marco. You must ask someone for the Rialto Bridge. Once there, you will find a clockmaker, I am sure of it."

He seized Julia by the wrist and leaned in close. "But be careful who you trust, my friends," he warned, eyes blazing. "In Venice there are thieves who will rob you, and criminals who will cut your throat."

Julia yanked her arm away.

"That's enough," Rick said, protectively stepping

between the boy and Julia. "We will be on our way. Thanks for your help."

The little dog watched forlornly as Rick and Julia crossed the street, distancing themselves from the beggars. Then, with a little yelp, it fled across the street to join them.

"Oh great," Rick groaned. "It looks like that flea-bag dog just adopted us."

"I think he's cute," Julia protested. "He just needs a bath."

Rick rolled his eyes to the sky. "I'm not touching him, that's all I know."

The three explorers walked in awestruck wonder along Venice's Grand Canal. The sight of so many boats on the water, combined with the astonishing buildings all around them, gave Julia a sense that she was traveling inside a dreamscape, a surreal world of great beauty. "I can't believe this is real," Julia whispered to Rick.

Jason stopped abruptly. He craned his neck, looking behind him. "They aren't there anymore," he said.

"Yeah, so?" Julia commented.

"The beggars," Jason said. "There were there . . . and now they've vanished."

"What's the big deal?" Julia asked.

A look of worry crossed Jason's face. "Guys," he confessed, "I was the last one through the door. I can't remember if I closed it or not."

"What?!" Rick exclaimed. The three immediately raced back in the direction of the door. There was no sign of the two street urchins anywhere.

Jason, Rick, and Julia entered the empty courtyard. "It can't be!" moaned Jason. "Please tell me they're still around here someplace."

Julia bent to pet the dog that had followed them faithfully. "Where are your owners, huh?" she asked.

Rick took a more thorough look around. "They're not here," he reported with growing concern.

The little dog sniffed the ground. It moved steadily away from Julia toward the archway that hid the Door to Time. The dog stopped at the door, looked back at Julia, and began to bark furiously.

"No! No! No! Please don't let it be so. . . !" Jason exclaimed. "I think they went to Kilmore Cove!"

Cornwall - England

Nestor felt exhausted, worn down by strain. He slowly climbed the staircase and stopped. He faced the door to the tower and saw a shadow reflected in the mirror.

"They are gone now," he said aloud. "It had to be done, no choice. True, they are only children. What chance do they have? But," he mused, "maybe they can find Peter. After all, they were able to open the door. Besides, there is no one else left. They're all dead or gone. These three children are our last hope."

Nestor coughed. He felt bone tired. He didn't know if he had the strength for this. "Perhaps I've been wrong," he mused, still facing the mirror. "Maybe it's best to leave things be." He shook his head sadly. Suddenly there was a bang on the floor below, the sound of a great door slamming shut.

"What's this, Esme?" exclaimed a male voice from below.

Nestor stiffened. A gust of wind hit his ankles. The window in the little tower flew open.

"Are we dreaming?" exclaimed a girl's voice below.

Nestor's mind reeled. He sought a weapon, some kind of protection, and grabbed a nearby walking stick.

He descended the stairs, ready for battle.

"Okay, Jason, just calm down and think about it for a minute," ordered Rick. "It doesn't help us if you freak out."

Jason anxiously paced back and forth, clearly doing exactly that — freaking out.

Julia turned to Rick. "What should we do?"

Rick spoke in calm tones. "All right, listen. Three of us came to Venice, but two returned to Kilmore Cove. Agreed?" said Rick.

"Yeah," Julia answered.

"That means only one of us can return," Rick reasoned.

Julia nodded. "Right. That's the way the door works. If three leave, only three can return. We learned that on our trip to Egypt."

"Argh! How could I have been so stupid!" Jason screamed.

Rick and Julia looked at each other. "So . . . who's going to go back?" Julia asked.

"It has to be either me or Jason," Rick stated. "It won't be easy getting those two back here from Argo Manor. It might take force."

Julia nodded. Rick was right.

"Whoever goes, one thing is for sure. That person can't fail," Rick continued, "or else the two who remain will never be able to return to Kilmore Cove."

Julia looked to her brother. "Jason and I should stay together," she said, unable to imagine a life without her twin.

"No, it has to be me," said Jason. "What happened was my fault. I'm the one who has to set it right."

Julia hesitated before giving her brother the four keys. "What if . . ."

"I won't fail," Jason vowed.

"You *can't*," Rick said. "Failure is not an option. Or else we'll be trapped here forever."

"I won't fail," Jason promised. "Meanwhile, don't forget why we came here in the first place. You guys still need to find Peter Dedalus."

Julia reached for Jason's arm. "Don't go," she pleaded.

"This is the only way," Jason answered. "Don't worry, Julia. I'll come back to get you. I'll meet you here at dusk."

Rick shook Jason's hand. "Good luck," he said.

Julia abruptly threw her arms around Jason's neck and kissed him on the cheek. "I love you, brother," she said.

"Most people do," Jason said with grin. Then he disappeared through the Door to Time.

Julia stood frozen, stunned, in the middle of the courtyard. Even with Rick at her side, she felt horribly alone. Her twin brother was gone, and here they were, foreigners in a city they didn't know, in a century they could scarcely conceive. An awkward silence surrounded them. Finally, it was Julia who broke it.

"Look, let's just find Dedalus and get back here as soon as we can," she said. "We'll have to trust that Jason can keep his part of the bargain."

Rick looked grim, serious. Maybe, Julia suspected, he was a little bit afraid. "Okay," he agreed. "Let's get out of here. We're wasting time."

They walked together out of the courtyard, over the bridge, and toward Saint Mark's Square. The dog followed behind, darting between their heels.

"He'll be okay, right?" Julia suddenly asked. Her eyes were moist, her tone doubtful.

Rick took her hand. "Yeah, everything's going to be fine," he promised.

Hi

After his return journey, Jason paused before pushing open the Door to Time. All during the trip, he had imagined a variety of scenarios that he might find. Perhaps Nestor was in hiding. Or perhaps the two urchins from Venice were sitting at the kitchen table, full of wide-eyed wonder, while Nestor served them tea! He also imagined scenes that were far worse, things gone horribly, horribly wrong.

Jason took a deep breath, promising himself that he'd be cautious, ready for anything. He pushed the door open.

Still hidden behind the armoire, Jason surveyed the stone room. It was empty. He sighed in relief. But then he heard the beggar boy's voice. It seemed to come from the terrace. Because of the magic of the doors, the words were in English.

"Stop struggling, old man, you can't get free from these ropes," the boy said. "I tied them nice and tight. Now tell me. Where are we?"

Jason heard Nestor's muffled voice. Jason couldn't understand the words.

The girl complained, "Diego, he can't answer your questions with that rag in his mouth."

"Shut up, Esme. I'll handle this!" Diego said.

Still alone in the empty room, Jason crept closer toward the voices. He heard the street boy tell Nestor, "Promise not to scream, old man. There's no one to hear you, anyway."

"I suggest you don't touch anything!" threatened Nestor, free from the restraining gag.

"Still trying to give orders, old man?" the beggar Diego mocked. "Do you not see that we are the ones in charge here?"

Heart pounding, Jason finally got a view of the intruders. They had tied up Nestor, who now sat on the sofa by the fireplace. The caretaker looked battered and bruised, as if he had been in a fight — and lost.

Diego stood before Nestor, interrogating him. "Is this your house?"

"No," answered the caretaker. He struggled against the ropes.

"Settle down, grandfather," warned Diego. "We don't want to hurt you. You attacked us, remember? If this is not your house, what are you doing here?"

"I'm the caretaker," Nestor answered.

"Very nice," Diego answered. "You see, my friend Esme and I live on the streets. We are not like you, old and fat from living the easy life."

"Where in Venice are we?" Esme asked. "I don't recognize this place."

"This is not Venice!" Nestor blurted out. "We're in England!"

"England? Is it part of Venice?" Esme wondered.

"Oh Lord!" moaned Nestor, frustrated.

"Bah! You talk nonsense, grandfather," Diego said. "We have many questions. First, we don't understand how we got here. Why doesn't the door open anymore?"

Nestor defiantly lifted his chin and shut his mouth. There was no point trying to explain it.

"Forget the old man," Esme said to Diego. "Let's take a look around."

"Yes," Diego agreed. "We'll see what's worth stealing."

Jason retreated behind a door seconds before the intruders passed. They climbed the stairs to the second floor.

Jason slipped silently onto the terrace.

Seeing him, Nestor's eyes became as big as saucers. "What are you doing here? Who are those two?"

"There was a problem," Jason whispered.

"Yes, I can see that," Nestor grumbled, wriggling under the ropes. "See if you can untie me. . . ."

"Ahhh!" screeched Esme from upstairs. "Flour on the floor! Why on earth?"

In spite of his predicament, the caretaker smiled. "I think those two found your ghost traps."

"Hurry up and let's get out of here," Jason said, helping Nestor to his feet.

"No," said Nestor. "I won't leave the house to those two!"

Jason bit his lip. "Do you have any bright ideas?"

Nestor's eyes twinkled. "Yes, in fact I do. Run to the lighthouse and get Leonard Minaxo!"

"Leonard Minaxo," the boy repeated.

"Tell him what happened," continued the caretaker. "Don't be afraid to talk to him, Jason. You can tell him everything. Leonard knows. He's on our side."

"He knows . . . what?" Jason asked doubtfully.

Another scream came from the top floor.

"Jason, please, I don't have time to explain. Run, now!" Nestor urged.

Jason went to the door of the terrace. He glanced back at Nestor apprehensively. "The ropes! I have to tie you back up!"

"There's no time," Nestor ordered. "I'll figure out something, it's not like we're dealing with rocket scientists. In the meantime, tell Leonard that we'll try the pigeon-in-the-well plan. He'll know what you mean."

Jason repeated, "The pigeon in the well. I got it — whatever it means."

The intruders' footsteps were on the stairs. "Go! Hurry!" Nestor whispered.

Jason fled the house with his heart pounding. The courtyard was quiet, the trees still. Jason saw Rick's bicycle on the gravel pathway. All he needed was to reach the bike unseen. He estimated the distance between himself and the bike, assessed the situation, and made his move.

He darted to the bike, turned it around, and raced off in one swift movement. He pedaled hard past the gate, past the white marble columns, to the windy cliff road. In the distance he saw the lighthouse at the far side of the bay.

Jason understood the urgency of his mission. He pedaled as if his life — and Nestor's — depended on it.

R ick and Julia set off in search of the Rialto Bridge, with the flea-bitten dog trotting behind them. They came to the square that the beggar had described to them. Rick admired the two stone columns that marked the entrance to the square. On top of one of the columns, the statue of a winged lion, the symbol of the city, reigned majestically.

The square was vibrant with the comings and goings of people wearing spectacular gowns, wigs, white stockings, and multicolored masks.

"Stay close," Rick whispered to Julia.

"Where's that bridge?" she asked.

Rick shrugged. He pointed to an enormous church. Beside it was a building with an immense clock. "Let's head that way," he suggested.

The tall, narrow building had an enormous clock with a golden dial. On the roof of the clock tower, the giant statues of two Moors marked the hour by striking a massive bell with their hammer. The base of the building had a large archway that allowed pedestrians to reach the hub of commercial Venice.

"Cool!" exclaimed Julia. "It's so huge I almost didn't see it! Do you think Peter built it?"

"I don't see any owls," answered the boy, studying the clock. Owls were Peter's trademark, like a signature.

Rick and Julia walked through the archway and found an arrow on the wall pointing to the Rialto Bridge. The large, open street transformed itself into a labyrinth of narrow streets crowded with people, shops, and open markets separated from each other by canals. Looking up, they gazed at the houses that seemed to be resting one against the other. Arcades and buttresses created a maze of passageways, elevated footbridges, and walkways where cascades of flowers, rugs, and colored coats of arms adorned edifices and bridges.

Following the flow of the crowd, Rick and Julia reached a small square. They steadily climbed the steps leading to a large white bridge, thickly set with magnificent shopping arcades. With elegance and seeming dignity, this bridge spanned the largest of all the Venetian canals, the Grand Canal.

They had arrived at the Rialto.

Under the span of the bridge, gondolas and boats glided past the gilded palaces that vainly reflected themselves on the Grand Canal. At the other end of the bridge an enormous open market was in full swing. Before them lay an entire street that seemed made to order: It was the street of the clockmakers.

Rick and Julia wandered tirelessly from store to

store asking for Peter Dedalus, but no one had heard of him.

Discouraged, they went back to the little market square where masons, busy chiseling blocks of stone, created tiny blue and purple sparks each time their chisel met the stone. The square was a hub-bub of dark-skinned slaves carrying large sacks of spices and other goods on their backs. Merchants welcomed potential customers into their rich stores with a promise of fantastic bargains. Exhausted, Julia and Rick sat next to the statue of a hunchback who, according to Ulysses Moore's journal, brought good luck.

"It's useless! We were crazy to think we could succeed. This place is too big!" Julia groaned. She absently caressed the little dog that had followed them through the thick maze of people.

"Got any bright ideas?" she asked Rick.

Rick flipped through the pages of Ulysses Moore's journal. "Not yet," he murmured without looking up. He was engrossed in reading. Finally he spoke up, "Look at this, Julia. Ulysses glued in an old comic strip."

"A cartoon?" she said. "What does it say? I could use a laugh right now."

Rick read from the journal:

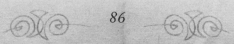

"*There are three magical places in Venice. The first is in the Calle Love of Friends, the second is near the Wonderland Bridge, and the third is in the Calle of the Converts near Saint Jeremiah in the Ghetto. When the Venetians are tired of the established authority, they go to these three secret places, open the doors at the edges of these courtyards, and travel to exotic places and other times.*"

"It looks like this cartoon is pointing to our doors!" exclaimed Julia.

"Yeah, I think so, too," agreed Rick. "But we didn't come out from any of these three places," he noted. "That suggests that there's at least four magical places in this city."

Rick handed the journal to Julia. He took out the map and began searching for the names mentioned in the journal.

"Bingo!" he said triumphantly. "I found Saint Jeremiah in the Ghetto as well as Wonderland Bridge. Unfortunately, they aren't close. On the other hand, Calle Love of Friends . . . well, I can't find it at all."

Julia flipped through the rest of Ulysses Moore's journal. "Hey, Rick! Look what he scribbled next to this photo!"

The snapshot was of an old Venetian house at the

edge of a canal. "*Old house in Saint Marina,*" Rick read. "So?"

"What do you mean, so?" Julia snapped. "Didn't you say that Penelope came from Venice?"

Rick looked at the photo again. A large tree obscured the main entrance. There was a crest painted on top of the entrance. A twisted lizard formed the letter *S*.

"Sauri . . ." whispered Rick. "Holy smoke! Could this be her old home?"

"Get the map," Julia said, excited and energized. "Where's Saint Marina?"

"It's not too far from here at all," said Rick. "We've only got to go a little farther up the road, make a left, and we should be there!"

The house looked different from the photo. It had been painted bright yellow. A floral crest in the shape of the letter *C* had replaced the lizard crest.

Rick banged on the door. Julia signaled for the dog — newly christened "Fleabag" by Rick — to be still.

The door opened, and a middle-aged man wearing a brown velvet suit appeared. His long jacket and leather vest had dark fur trimmings; his trousers were gathered below the knees by white stockings, and his black shoes sported golden buckles. He had piercing eyes, a long mustache, and a short, white wig.

The man eyed the visitors with suspicion. "May I help you?" he asked.

"We don't mean to bother you, sir," Rick hastily said. "We were wondering if you knew . . ."

"I'm sorry, children," the man interrupted. "But I believe you have come to the wrong door."

"Ulysses and Penelope Moore!" Julia spoke up, finishing Rick's sentence.

The man's eyebrows shot up in surprise. "That name!" he gasped. "How . . . what do you . . . know of the Moores?"

The door opened ever so slightly.

"It's a long story, sir," Julia continued. "You see, we live in Ulysses Moore's house and, um, thanks to him we were able to come to Venice in a very unconventional, um, totally weird way." Julia looked to Rick for encouragement. "I don't know if I'm explaining myself well. . . ."

For the first time, a flicker of a smile crossed the man's face. "Truthfully, young miss, I have no idea what you just said. However, I will admit some degree of surprise, because we are the ones who live in Ulysses Moore's house." He paused. "Where exactly are you from?"

"From Cornwall, sir," answered Rick. "England."

An expression of astonishment filled his face.

"Alberto, who is at the door?" said a voice from inside the house. A much younger woman with a cascade of black curls, rosy cheeks, and lively eyes came to the door. "Hello," she said warmly when she saw Rick and Julia. "Who are you?"

Fleabag stepped toward the raven-haired woman, yelping excitedly.

The man cast a look of contempt at the motley dog. "This is my wife, Rosella Caller. My name is Alberto. Let's continue our conversation inside, away from prying eyes. Please, this way," he gestured. "But I must request that you leave this shaggy, flea-bitten creature outside."

The children were escorted through a narrow, high-ceilinged hallway that was jammed with marvelous furniture and paintings. They crossed the dining room and came to an inner courtyard that was brimming with ivy and tall, cylindrical trees that reached to the sky.

Alberto Caller sat and gestured for his guests to

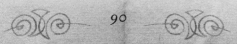

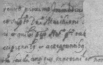

do the same. He said to his wife, "These children claim they are from England and that they are guests at the house of Ulysses Moore."

Rosella smiled. "Oh really? It has been such a long time since we've seen them! Tell me, children, how are the Moores?"

Julia and Rick exchanged a look. Rick bit his lip. "To be honest, both of them have passed away."

Both of the Callers' faces saddened. "Oh dear," Rosella murmured. "We're so sorry. Had you known them long?"

Julia answered, "We've actually never met them."

"I don't understand," Alberto said. His tone was still formal, stiff, and decidedly unfriendly.

"Alberto, your manners, please," Rosella scolded.

"Dear," he rejoined, "I am simply trying to comprehend how these young strangers came to knock on our door. You know very well we don't allow many people to come into our house."

"Oh, Alberto, you are too suspicious!" Rosella said, smiling at Julia and Rick. "Just one glance and I can tell you that these are nice children."

Alberto had no reaction. "Are you related to Ulysses?" he inquired.

"No, sir," Julia responded. "After the Moores died, my parents bought their house in England.

When we moved there, we found some things that belonged to them, including this journal. . . ."

She handed Alberto the travel journal.

"I remember these journals," Rosella stated.

"Were you friends with Ulysses Moore?" Rick asked.

Alberto nodded.

"What kind of a person was he?" Rick probed. "I mean, physically. What did he look like?"

"Oh, a fine-looking gentleman," Rosella replied. "Tall, elegant, imposing."

"Come now, Rosella," Alberto said with a trace of jealousy. "He was hardly imposing!"

"And what about Penelope, um, Mrs. Moore?" Julia asked. "I imagine her as a beautiful woman."

"Penelope was sweetness itself," Rosella answered. "A good soul, intelligent, and refined. When she lived in this house, before moving abroad, Penelope hosted the most marvelous parties. An invitation from Penelope was the most prized invitation in Venice. And yet she was simple, without pretense or aristocratic ways."

"She was stunning!" added Alberto.

"Ah!" snapped Rosella playfully.

Alberto ran his fingertips across his mustache. "Not as beautiful as you, my dear," he said, eyes

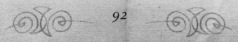

twinkling, "but one could not help but notice Penelope's considerable charms."

Rosella rose from her seat. She winked at Julia. "Julia, let us leave these two for a moment. Please, come with me. I have something I'd like to show you."

"Alberto won't tolerate servants," Rosella confided to Julia. "We had a bad experience with our last servant, so now he doesn't trust anyone to come into the house." After a brief pause, she added, "He's not all that wrong, you know."

Julia listened without comment. She followed Rosella upstairs.

"Wait here a moment, please," Rosella told Julia when they came to a door. "No one has been inside this room for some time. I'm afraid it might be quite musty."

It was a bedroom with a marble floor. At the foot of the bed stood a small, round table covered with elegant jewelry boxes. There was also a washstand, an oval mirror, and a flowered porcelain bowl.

"Penelope's room?" Julia guessed.

Rosella smiled. "Yes, you are very perceptive, Julia. When Alberto and I came to live here, we decided to leave this room as it was."

Julia took a few hesitant steps into the room. She stopped before a large oil painting.

"Is that her?" she asked in a whisper. "Penelope?"

"Yes. I must admit that Alberto was correct. Penelope was indeed beautiful," answered Rosella.

Julia stared at the painting, speechless. It awed her to finally see Penelope's picture, here in Venice. It

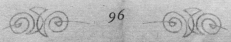

served as a mysterious link between two worlds. Across time and space.

The painting depicted a girl with long, light hair gathered together by a ribbon. She stood near an open window, the same window that was in arm's reach of Julia right now. Staring at the picture, Julia lost herself in Penelope's gaze. Somehow, Julia felt a connection to her. A kinship.

"You look like her," Rosella noted. "Sisters, almost. That's why I wanted to show this painting to you."

Yes, that was it, Julia thought. Staring at Penelope Moore, it was as if . . . she were looking into a mirror.

Alberto called up the stairs. Instantly, the room's spell was broken.

"Oh, ladies!" he called. "Have you abandoned us forever?"

Rosella laughed happily. "Men," she said, "the most helpless creatures on earth!"

Alberto turned his attention back to Rick. "So that's the whole story," he concluded, rising to greet his wife and Julia. "We've been here ever since."

Rick explained to Julia, "Alberto was telling me that the Sauri family became extinct when Penelope took Moore as a surname," he explained. "The family ended right there."

"Ended!" Julia said. She thought of the painting in the bedroom upstairs. The kinship she felt staring into Penelope's gray eyes. "You mean there was no one else left to carry on the family name?"

"Correct," Alberto said. "There was almost a brawl in the city when it became known that Penelope had fallen in love with a stranger. A foreigner, to boot," he continued.

Signor Caller smoothed his mustache. "You have not yet told us why you've come to Venice. It is, after all, a long way from England."

"We are looking for someone," Rick answered. "An old friend of Ulysses Moore. We thought that maybe he was your friend, too. His name was, I mean, his name *is* . . . Peter Dedalus."

Rick's words hung in the air like smoke. Time passed without either of the Callers giving the smallest hint of recognition.

"Dedalus, you say?" Alberto finally said. He frowned, glancing at his wife. "I've never heard that name. Have you, Rosella?"

She shook her head. "No, I'm sorry. I don't know anyone who goes by that name."

"Peter is something of a genius," Rick explained. "An inventor, a clockmaker, in fact." He rummaged

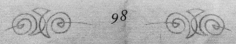

through his backpack, looking for his wristwatch. He handed it to Alberto.

Signor Caller viewed it with fascination. "A wristwatch, you say?" he commented. "I have never seen anything like it in all my life."

Rick pointed out the owl design on the watch face. "It's sort of his signature," Rick explained. "Peter loves owls."

"Oh, but of course!" exclaimed Rosella. "I've seen an owl like this before — an owl engraved on top of a box. Isn't that right, Alberto?"

"Perhaps, but it's not a clock, my dear," Signor Caller replied.

"True," Rosella answered, undeterred, "but it was Penelope's. . . ."

Julia remembered Nestor's last words before the Door to Time closed behind them. "Don't forget that Peter was crazy about music!" Nestor had said.

"Was it a music box?" she asked.

Rosella looked at Julia with surprise. "Yes, a music box — that's it!" she exclaimed. "Would you like to see it?"

"Yes, please!" Rick answered.

Everyone stood and followed Rosella out of the room, energized by this new clue. Rick whispered to Julia, "What's the matter with you? You've been acting weird since you returned from upstairs."

"Well, yeah, duh," Julia replied. "Didn't you notice anything?"

"Notice what?"

"Penelope."

"What about her?" Rick asked.

"They said that the Sauri family name ended in 1751," Julia said. "Penelope was the last of the line."

Rick thought about it for a moment. When the lightbulb went on, he stopped in his tracks. Of course! *If Penelope Sauri's family name ended in 1751, it meant that Penelope was born in the eighteenth century.*

Ulysses Moore must have traveled through time to marry her.

- Chapter 14 -
RACE TO THE
LIGHTHOUSE

Pedaling hard, Jason climbed the hill on the opposite side of the bay. He left the main road behind and turned onto the narrow path that led to the lighthouse. The peninsula was long and narrow. The sea hammered both of its sides where the meadow extended toward the sea. The wind slapped the waves against the shore with brutal force. The seagulls floated overhead, almost motionless in all that wind, like a mobile above an infant's crib.

Fighting against the cold wind, Jason neared the lighthouse. It was taller than he had expected, now that he was seeing it up close for the first time. The only door appeared to be locked by an iron latch. Jason shielded his eyes with his hand and looked about. There didn't seem to be any way inside. No doorbell or intercom.

He walked around the lighthouse, and then headed to the lighthouse keeper's cottage, a simple building that appeared devoid of light.

"Mr. Minaxo!" Jason yelled. "Mr. Minaxo!"

He came to the front door and called out again. No one answered. Jason peered through a window and saw a table with a knife on it, a sink, and an old wooden stove. There was no sign of Leonard Minaxo.

Suddenly Jason sensed a shadow, a nearby presence, and spun around. He squinted into the sun and saw a man with long hair. He held a harpoon in his grip.

"Who are you?" the man boomed.

Jason felt his throat tighten. He fought the impulse to retreat. But Nestor had sent him there. . . . Jason had to hold his ground.

"Are you Leonard?" he asked.

A black patch covered the man's right eye. The good eye was icy blue. He had a pointed nose and broad shoulders, and wore a shark's tooth around his neck.

He stabbed the harpoon into the ground. "I asked first," the man stated.

"I'm Jason," he answered. "I'm looking for Leonard Minaxo."

"Why would you be looking for Leonard?" the man queried.

"Nestor sent me," Jason answered. "He said that you are on our side."

The man scowled. "Explain yourself!"

Jason took a deep breath. "First, I have to know: Are you Leonard?"

"You've got guts, kid," the man said. He pushed past Jason and opened the door to the house.

"Yeah, I'm Leonard," he said. "Don't just stand there with your mouth open, boy. Hurry up, step out of the wind."

Leonard Minaxo gestured for Jason to sit on a wooden stool. He carelessly threw the harpoon on the table, removed his shirt, and turned on the water at the sink. While washing his hands and arms, Leonard asked, "Why did Nestor send you here?"

"Nestor is in danger," Jason answered. "He said you could help him."

"What do you mean, in danger?" Leonard asked, shutting off the faucet, turning to give Jason his full attention.

"He said that the two of you needed to try, um, something called . . . the pigeon-in-the-well plan," Jason said.

Leonard tilted his head to the side. "He said that, did he?"

Jason nodded. "He's being held captive by two street beggars."

"Street beggars? In Kilmore Cove?!" Leonard said, incredulous.

"I don't know what they are," Jason said. "Thieves, or whatever. They came to Argo Manor and they tied up Nestor."

"They came to Argo Manor, huh?" Leonard said,

his ice-blue eye coldly calculating. "Came from where, exactly?"

Jason shrugged, not ready to reveal that much.

The lighthouse keeper nodded his head, studying Jason intently, as if weighing something in his mind.

"He said that you'd know what to do," Jason said, urgency in his voice. "We don't have time to waste. Nestor said we could trust you."

The lighthouse keeper frowned. He grabbed the harpoon from the table and, in the same motion, tossed a knife at Jason.

"Do you know how to use a knife, boy?" he asked.

Jason caught the knife, surprised at his own reflexes. "Sure," he lied.

"Knives are a simple business," Leonard said. "You just stick it in and twist. Now let's go."

Leonard strode out of the house, with Jason hurrying after.

"What's the pigeon-in-the-well plan?" Jason asked.

"The well is in Turtle Park," Leonard answered.

Jason shook his head. Turtle Park! Where the Moore Mausoleum is located.

Leonard reached a small barn and unbolted the door. He threw open the door and went in. Speaking with surprising tenderness, the gruff man cooed, "Come, pretty one. We're going out!"

Jason remained at the door. He stared at a magnificent horse with a dark satiny torso and a white mane. Leonard stroked the horse on the nose. "How do you fare with horses?" he asked Jason.

"I've never been on one," Jason admitted.

The lighthouse keeper grinned. "There's always a first time."

"Actually, um," Jason said, his heart pounding at the thought, "I have my bike here."

"Come," Minaxo demanded.

Jason walked hesitantly into the stable. The horse took him in with one round eye that loomed above Jason.

"Allow me to make introductions," Leonard said. "Ariadne, this young whelp is named Jason — and he needs a ride." The man gestured for Jason to stroke Ariadne's face. "There, now you're friends."

Jason tried to protest. He had never been on a horse in his life and, quite frankly, he was in no hurry to rectify that situation.

Diego Valente, the street urchin from Venice, stared into the refrigerator, entranced by its "magical light." The girl, Esme, moved around the house, examining everything she came across. If she decided the object had value, Esme placed it with other items that she had piled haphazardly by the front door. The two beggars had decided to steal as much as they could carry.

"Thieves," Nestor muttered with contempt.

Diego shrugged. "Borrowers, actually," he said. "These are just things. Once yours, now ours. One day they will be someone else's. And so the world goes round and round."

"I don't care what you call it," Nestor said. "It is still stealing."

"Okay," Diego said, smiling happily. "Whatever you say, old man. You have so much, while Esme and I have so little. We live on the streets like dogs, while you have this beautiful house filled with riches. Tell me, old man, is that fair? Is that justice? Are we the thieves? Or are you?"

"Where do you come from? Are you Spanish?" Nestor asked.

"I am a citizen of the world," Diego answered. "My mother was born in Valencia. My father . . . who knows? He died long ago. At age twelve, I boarded a ship, never to return home again. I went to Greenland, Marseilles, Genoa . . . many places. I met Esme and we traveled to Venice. And now, today, we are here with you, old man."

Nestor watched as Esme continued to pile up his belongings. "Take it all," he said scornfully. "But go. Go now!"

Diego paused before the enormous quantity of items that Esme had gathered. He scratched his head. "We need a horse," he said.

"There is no stable at Argo Manor," Nestor replied. "However, there may be one possibility. . . ."

"What is it? Do you know where we can get a horse?" Diego asked.

Nestor feigned reluctance. His plan was working, but he had to pretend otherwise. "I won't tell you," he finally said, as if tormented by the thought of helping his captors. "The owner of this house would never forgive me."

Diego picked up a knife and stepped toward Nestor. "You must tell us where to find a horse," he threatened Nestor, "or your blood will spill on the floor."

Nestor smiled inwardly. Diego had fallen into his trap. "Please, no violence," Nestor said. "If you insist, I will help you find a horse."

R osella and Alberto Caller led Julia and Rick to a remarkable painting.

"Rick!" Julia exclaimed. "That's Argo Manor!"

"What did you say?" Alberto asked.

"That's where we live!" Julia answered. "The garden, the cliffs, the gate. That's our home."

"Very interesting," Rosella said. "Alberto, show them the frame."

Alberto hauled over a nearby chair. He took off his shoes, stood on the chair, and carefully lifted the painting from the wall.

Stepping off the chair, Signor Caller turned the painting around to reveal a small handle that was concealed behind the golden frame. The design of an owl was engraved on the metal cylinder, which was attached to the handle by a wheel capped with small metallic points.

"Listen . . ." Alberto whispered. He turned the handle. A haunting melody filled the room.

Upon hearing the music, Rick was instantly transported back to his childhood. It was the same melody that he had heard years ago when he and his father used to visit Peter's shop in Kilmore Cove. Rick had no doubt that it was the same music. It was ingrained in his memory, a cherished part of his childhood.

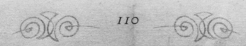

"It's Peter's music," Rick declared in a whisper. "I recognize it."

"We will help you find him," Alberto announced.

Rosella nodded enthusiastically. "We will join your adventure and unravel the mystery of Peter Dedalus!"

"It won't be easy," Alberto noted. "Venice is a large city."

"True." Rick nodded thoughtfully. "The fact is, Peter does not wish to be found."

"What?" Rosella said.

"We believe that Peter came to Venice to hide . . . to run away," Julia explained. "He left a confession before he departed. He said that he wished to make a new life for himself, far from everyone."

"In that case, why don't you honor the man's wishes?" Alberto asked.

"We believe that Peter holds an important secret," Rick answered. "And we are not the only ones who are looking for him."

Alberto stroked his mustache thoughtfully. "The only thing we have of his is this clue: a painting and a frame."

"Earlier today, in Kilmore Cove, I found a sheet that said that to use the proper key and write DEDA if we wished to contact him," Rick said hesitantly. "Does that make any sense to you?"

"The proper key?" Rosella echoed.

"It sounds like that's some sort of puzzle," Alberto pondered.

"Yes, it's like a code of some sort," Julia said. "Peter spoke in riddles. He left behind incomprehensible clues."

"Bizarre, bizarre," Alberto mused to himself. "An inventor of clocks who hides in Venice . . . a man with a passion for music . . . and who leaves a message that makes no sense."

"I have an idea," Rosella announced. "Grab your capes. We are going to Saint Mary of Mercy's Hospital."

The little group quickly left the house. Alberto closed the front door with a huge key. He hung it around his neck and let the key slide under his vest. He handed the painting to his wife, then tucked something wrapped in cloth under his arm.

They quickly walked along the canal and crossed over to the Calle of Herbs.

"Near Saint Mary of Mercy's Hospital, there's the famous musical academy," she said. "Our own Antonio Vivaldi taught there recently."

"The man who wrote *The Four Seasons*?" Julia asked.

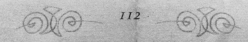

"Correct," Alberto confirmed, happily humming a few bars of the score.

"Since this music box is the only clue we have," Rosella explained, "it may be helpful if we can discover the name of the melody it plays."

Alberto smiled, finally understanding his wife's plan. "And who else could tell us this but the teachers at the best school in the city?"

They paused outside the school's gates. Alberto placed a cautionary hand on Rick's chest. "No," Alberto said, "only women may enter. It is the law."

"Why?" Julia asked.

"The school is strictly for women," Rosella said. "The young students learn to sing and play the violin, but they keep themselves hidden from the public eye by staying behind the gate."

Rick shook his head. "What is it with this place? Secret masks and mysterious costumes. What is everyone in this city trying to hide?"

Alberto glanced at Rosella, who returned his gaze in silence.

"A mask hides only the outside face," he stated. "The greatest secrets are hidden in the heart."

Rick and Alberto waited outside the gate while the women went inside to inquire about the song. Rick's thoughts turned to Jason . . . and Nestor . . .

and Kilmore Cove. The sun was dropping closer to the horizon. The sky had hues of gold and orange. So much of the day was gone, but they did not seem any closer to finding Peter.

Rick waited hopefully for Julia and Rosella's return, but seeing the expression on their faces when they came out of the academy, he realized at once they had not found out anything new.

Julia shook her head. "Nothing," she whispered to Rick. "Not one of the teachers had ever heard it. I think that means this song must have been written afterward."

"Afterward?" Rick asked.

"In our time," Julia said. "After the eighteenth century."

"So we've just dug a hole in the water?" Alberto sighed.

"Not necessarily," answered Rosella with a smile. She handed him a sheet of paper. "One of the teachers gave us the address of a man he thinks *might* have made this frame."

They came once again to Saint Mark's Square. Ladies strolled the streets dressed in magnificent gowns. The splendor of their attire combined with

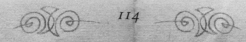

the beauty of the city made Julia feel as if she was walking through an unbelievable dream.

Heedless of her surroundings, Rosella led the way, chattering happily, steering her husband toward their destination.

Alberto stopped. "Ah, wait a moment, please. We must stop for a treat." He told Rick and Julia, "You cannot visit our fair city without tasting a dessert from Cafe Florian."

Alberto took Rick and Julia into a shop under one of the arched galleries that lined the square. The choices were astounding: innumerable flower-flavored waters, lemonades, ices, cones, ice creams, sorbets, and, most notably, vanilla-flavored chocolate sweets. Alberto paid for four treats that were served warmed in a paper cone. Yet when it was time to leave the cafe, his face suddenly darkened. "Count Ashes," he whispered.

He took Rosella's hand. She froze in place, a look of fear on her face. "Perhaps he didn't see us," she said.

The Callers suddenly turned their backs on the square and faced the children.

"What's the matter?" Rick asked. "You look like you've seen a ghost."

Alberto smiled stiffly. "An unfortunate

encounter, I'm afraid," he answered, nervously clutching the package under his arms. "Rick, would you do me a favor, please? There's no time to explain." He handed the package to Rick. "I need you to hold this for me. There is a person here who, well, could cause us all a great deal of difficulty."

Rick nodded and took the package.

Alberto put a hand on Rick's shoulder. "Please do this," he instructed. "Walk under the gallery and proceed straight until you see a church called Saint Moses. It will give us time to get rid of this man. We will meet you there."

Rick instinctively trusted Alberto and Rosella, though he did not know what was concealed in the cloth bundle. It was lighter than he had imagined. With Julia at his side, Rick hurried in the direction of the church.

"Count Ashes," Oblivia Newton said in greeting to the masked man outside Cafe Florian.

The secret guard nodded to Oblivia, but kept his eyes on the two people before him. "Ah, Ms. Newton," Count Ashes purred. "How nice to see you again. I was just chatting with two of my dear friends . . . Rosella and Alberto Caller.

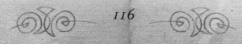

"Signor Caller was once a most excellent, learned man," continued the count, stressing the past tense of the verb, "before moving to his new residence."

Trying to change the subject, Rosella interjected, "Are you from Venice, Signora Newton? I don't believe we've met before."

"No, I am from out of town," Oblivia answered. "However, the Count has been kind enough to serve as my guide."

"Very well." Alberto smiled. "We were just about to take our leave. Count, our regards and best wishes."

With a quick bow, Alberto and Rosella hastily left.

"Go on with your little games. . . ." hissed Count Ashes as the couple walked away. "Soon you will have to answer to The Council of Ten."

"Sounds delicious," Oblivia purred behind her mask. "What have those two done to invite such scorn?"

"They are illuminati," the count replied with a wave of his hand. "They disseminate forbidden books. It is only a matter of time before I catch them in the act."

"Ah, yes, well, forbidden books. How dangerous," Oblivia said sarcastically. "Today we are meeting for a different purpose. Do you have what I need?"

Without speaking, the count moved swiftly through the square. The thick crowd seemed to open a path for him as he passed.

"Did you find him?" Oblivia asked.

"Did you bring my money?" Count Ashes replied.

Oblivia jingled the coins under her cape. Behind his mask, the count smiled. Easy money. He led her to a bell tower that featured a huge clock at its zenith.

Count Ashes entered the tower. "Come quickly," he hissed.

"But where are . . . ?"

"Silence," the count demanded. He led her to a room with an old wooden staircase.

"I don't understand," Oblivia complained.

Count Ashes held out the palm of his hand. "The money, Ms. Newton."

"Before I give you anything," Oblivia stated, "first tell me about Peter. Did you find him or not?"

Count Ashes bowed slightly. "Of course, although now he goes by another name. These days he calls himself Peter Englishman."

"Peter Englishman," Oblivia repeated.

"He is a clockmaker," Count Ashes informed her. "And, I gather, quite clever at it — or so they say."

"Yes, yes," Oblivia said impatiently. "But where is he?"

The count pointed his index finger to the ceiling. "At this very moment, he is repairing the clock tower above us. You need only to climb these stairs."

Oblivia placed a small sack of coins into the man's hands. And without another word, she turned to climb the stairs, like a lioness stalking her prey.

Rick and Julia sat on the front steps of the church. Rick held the cloth bundle in his lap. "I think we should look inside," he told Julia.

Julia bit her lip, uncertain.

Rick continued, "You saw the look on Alberto's face. After he saw that masked man, he couldn't get rid of this package fast enough."

"It could be something illegal," Julia said.

Rick nodded. "That's right. We don't know what we're carrying. And the truth is, we don't know much about Alberto and Rosella Caller."

"They seem so nice," Julia protested.

"Yes," Rick agreed. "They *seem* that way. Still, I

don't feel right carrying a package when I don't know what's inside it."

Julia looked torn. But finally, she nodded her head slowly.

Rick opened the package. A puzzled expression crossed his face. "It's . . . a book."

"Weird," Julia commented.

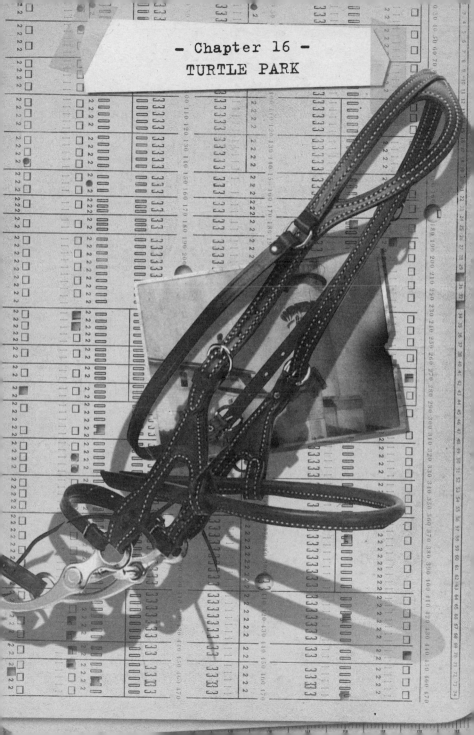

Leonard hitched Ariadne to an old cart while Jason watched, hoping to learn something about how to behave around horses. A moment later Leonard and Jason were seated side by side, while Ariadne pulled the cart along a gravel road.

Jason looked behind him. The cart held an old fishing net and a long coil of rope. "What's that stuff for?" he asked Leonard.

The lighthouse keeper spit in reply.

"So," Jason said, "I guess you don't like to talk much."

Leonard grunted. He paused, then finally said, "I'm not all that keen on listening, either." But after a while he added, "Not much farther now, you'll see soon enough. Let's just hope that Nestor holds up his end of the bargain."

"His end?" Jason asked.

Leonard looked straight ahead, steering the cart down a dusty path. "He's got to deliver the pigeons."

They came down the hill and circled the bay, past the place where the old train station used to be. They crossed the tracks and began to ascend a narrow trail. The horse worked tirelessly, neither fast nor slow. The vegetation grew thicker and denser. They came to a clearing with tall trees on either side, and passed under a wrought-iron archway covered with flowering vines.

"Turtle Park," Leonard murmured.

"It looks abandoned," Jason observed. He saw that the lawn had not been cut, the gardens were overrun, and the stone walkways appeared broken and disheveled.

Leonard frowned. "When this park was planned two hundred years ago, it was intended to be a botanical garden, hosting plants from all over the world. At some point I suppose the money dried up, because they stopped caring for it decades ago. Nothing is trimmed or cut or cared for. The funny thing is, I think it looks more beautiful this way."

"Who planned the park?" Jason wondered, rapt in the majesty of some of the exotic plants, the climbing vines, tall trees, and the wild vegetation that had reclaimed the paths.

"It was one of my, er, one of Mr. Moore's ancestors," Leonard replied.

"What?" Jason said immediately. "One of *your* ancestors, or one of Mr. Moore's?"

Leonard looked at Jason with a mocking smile. "Oh, you are a clever one, aren't you? One of Mr. Moore's ancestors, like I just said."

"No, you said . . ." Jason pressed.

"I said what I'm saying to you now, lad," Leonard interrupted. "The man's name was Raymond Moore. He was Ulysses Moore's great-great-grandfather, or something like it."

"Wow," Jason said. "Are you telling me that Mr. Moore's ancestors have lived in Kilmore Cove for hundreds of years?"

"Where else could they have lived?" Leonard snapped. "Piccadilly Circus or some other such foolishness?"

They came to an unusual monument: three stone turtles, one next to the other.

"I've seen those before," Jason remarked. They were the same turtles that were engraved above the door of the grotto in Salton Cliff.

Leonard cast his eyes sideways. "They are the same as the ones over the great door," he said.

"So you've seen it," Jason said, surprised.

"Talk, talk, talk," Leonard muttered. "Too much talk, don't you agree, Ariadne?"

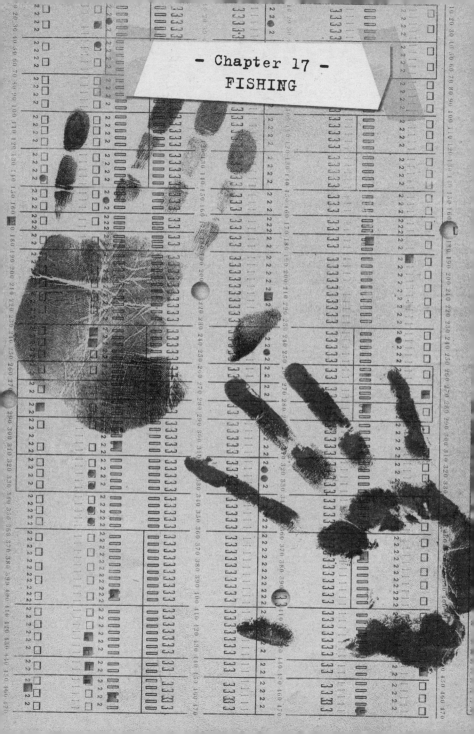

- Chapter 17 -
FISHING

Leonard and Jason continued deeper into the park. Jason could glimpse the ocean between breaks in the tree line, as well as the dark roofs of the houses of Kilmore Cove.

"Did you know Ulysses Moore?" he asked.

Leonard turned to look fully upon his inquisitor. "Do you not have ears, lad? Have you not learned that I prefer not to talk about it?"

Jason persisted. His curiosity was too great. "But why can't you answer a few simple questions? I have a right to know. I'm one of the good guys."

Leonard remained silent, fingering the reins in his hands.

"What was he like?" Jason asked.

"Ulysses was not one to sit around," Leonard said. "He was stubborn as the day is long. You could never tell that man what to do. That was his big problem, if you ask me. He wouldn't listen to sense."

"Did you two have a fight?" Jason asked.

"Enough chatter," Leonard said. He turned away.

"I'm on your side!" Jason exclaimed. "Why is everything a big, dark secret with you guys? I'm on Nestor's side, exactly like you."

"Tell me this," the lighthouse keeper said. "Did you travel?"

Jason was silent. Leonard's question meant only one thing: Did Jason ever sail the *Metis*? Did he ever cross the sea of time?

"Yes," Jason confessed.

"Alone?"

"I was with my sister, Julia, and Rick Banner," Jason told him.

"Where did you go?" Leonard shot back.

"We went to Egypt," Jason said. "And Venice — but things went wrong." Jason paused, deciding whether to press on. "What about you?" he finally asked.

Leonard did not answer. But Jason felt the truth in his bones. The lighthouse keeper had traveled through the door. He knew far more than he told. Leonard not only kept the lighthouse, he kept secrets, too.

"What did you see in Egypt?" Leonard asked.

"I was in the Land of Punt," Jason answered, "searching for the Room That Isn't There."

Leonard snorted. "And did you find it?"

"Yes, we did," Jason said, watching for Leonard's reaction. "We also found a map that Ulysses Moore had hidden there. But then Oblivia Newton stole it from us."

Leonard nodded slowly, as if deep in thought. "And what went wrong in Venice?" he asked.

"We went there to look for Peter Dedalus," Jason said. "But somehow two beggars passed through the door."

Leonard turned and stared at Jason with disapproval. "Very sloppy," he said. "I suppose that's why I'm here, isn't it? To clean up your mess?"

Jason did not reply.

"Nestor made some mistakes," Leonard grumbled.

"If you're referring to us, he didn't make a mistake!" Jason snapped back. "We found out everything by ourselves and . . ."

"Oh, really?" Leonard scoffed. "With no help at all? I find that hard to believe."

Jason gritted his teeth. "Respectfully, Mr. Minaxo, I don't care what you believe."

They came to a small, dilapidated house. "We're here, lad." Leonard Minaxo stopped the cart.

Jason looked around. They had climbed almost to the top of the hill. At their right, between the trees, they could see Argo Manor. "What now?" Jason asked.

Leonard climbed down from the cart. He started to haul off the heavy fishing net. "We get ready for the pigeons," he replied.

The house was almost completely obscured

beneath climbing vines and ramshackle vegetation. Leonard bent low under an archway. Jason followed him inside. The interior of the house was stark, lit by shafts of sunlight that came in from the windows and cracks in the roof. Smoke and cinders darkened the walls. There was also writing on the walls, drawn with pieces of coal.

"It's been donkey's years since I've been here," Leonard said.

"What is this place?" Jason asked.

"When I was your age," Leonard answered, "we used it as our secret hideaway."

Jason studied the handprints on the wall. He decided that they were from the hands of several children. He tried to read some of the writing, most of which had become blurred over time. With a thump of his heart he recognized the symbols that had been used in the Phaistos Disk mixed on the wall along with the standard letters of the alphabet. He had first learned about the symbols from the *Dictionary of Forgotten Languages*. It was just a few days ago, amazingly, before they had even known about the existence of the Door to Time.

Incredulous, Jason brushed over the strange symbols with his fingers. "Do you know these symbols?" he asked Leonard.

"It was our secret alphabet," the man said. He gestured to the wall and read: '*Of dreams we are but simple sailors, not . . .*'"

Jason continued, "'*. . . captains, anchors, or vessels.*'"

The lighthouse keeper looked at Jason with genuine surprise. He shook his head and stepped out into the air.

Jason paused inside, looking at the writing on the wall. He found Ulysses Moore's name, written with an unsteady hand, less refined than the penmanship he had learned to recognize in the manuscripts. Penelope's name was not there. He read the words, "*The great summer.*" Beneath it were three legible signatures: Peter, Nessa, and Black. A fourth signature that had been almost entirely erased by time, or by some other hand, followed the three names.

What were those names doing together? Jason wondered. If Peter was the clockmaker, and Nessa was Cleopatra Biggles' sister, then who was Black? Shivering, Jason looked at the prints on the walls of the secret house. How many years had gone by since they put the prints there? How many decades?

"Hey, laddie!" Leonard called from outside. "Am I to do all the work?"

"You didn't sign it," Jason noted, as he stepped outdoors.

"My signature must have gotten erased," Leonard muttered.

"Tell me about the great summer," Jason said.

Leonard permitted himself a smile. "Ah, it was truly a great summer. . . ." he reflected. "It was the summer when Ulysses first came here. The summer when our group formed."

"And then what happened?" Jason asked.

"Then summer ended, as all summers do," Leonard answered. "Autumn comes, then winter. Things wither and die. We were never the same again."

Leonard and Jason dragged the fishing net to a stone patio at the rear of the house. In the center was a rusted grating that covered the opening of a well. The lighthouse keeper grabbed the grate with two strong hands, pulled with all his strength, and lifted it up.

"What's down there?" Jason asked, peering into the darkness.

"Our pigeons," Leonard said with a wink. "At least, they will be soon enough. Your job will be to throw the net down on their heads."

Leonard continued talking, warming to the subject. "We explored it years ago, led by our good friend Black. Oh, Black was a brave one for that sort of thing — caves and dark tunnels and such.

Black always led the way. We called him the Black Volcano. Below this hole we found a vast network of caves."

Jason nodded. "I'm still confused about our plan," he said.

"Do you see that path, lad?" Leonard pointed out. "When Nestor told you that he wanted to try the pigeon-in-the-well plan, that means he'll arrive from there and enter the cave that's right below us."

Jason looked at the fishing net. "Oh, I get it," he said.

"When I give you the signal," Leonard advised Jason, "it's bombs away."

Not far away, Nestor plodded along with Diego and Esme. "How much farther?" the girl complained.

Diego threw down the bundle of stolen goods he carried on his shoulder, straightened his back, and stretched. "She's right, old man!" Diego said to Nestor. "Where is this horse?"

His hands bound by rope, Nestor gestured with a tilt of his head to a clearing ahead. "Just a few more steps," he urged. "I can already see the cave."

Diego looked suspiciously at Nestor. "A stable in a cave?"

"You asked me to take you to the nearest stable, not the best," Nestor replied. "If you'd prefer, we can go down to town. . . ."

Diego frowned. "You won't trick me, old man. We'll stay far away from the prying eyes in town. Come, let's go to your cave."

At that moment, they heard a horse whinny.

"There it is!" exclaimed Nestor with satisfaction. "Like I said, the horse is only steps away."

They entered the dark, damp cave. The inside smelled like sulfur. Esme looked doubtfully to Diego. "I don't like it here," she said.

"Who goes there?" called a voice from deeper inside the cave.

When their eyes adjusted to the darkness, Diego and Esme made out an imposing man standing beside a dark horse.

Nestor started to answer, but Diego cut him off.

"Horses," the boy said. "We are looking for two strong horses."

"Horses? Yes, I have horses," Leonard answered. "Come closer and choose one yourself."

The two beggars came closer to Leonard. One step, then another. Leonard watched and waited, thinking, *closer, closer, almost there, just another step* . . .

"NOW!" Leonard yelled.

Hearing the cry, Jason heaved the fishing net into the hole. In a moment, it fell with great force onto the heads of the two thieves, knocking them to the ground.

Jason sprinted down the path to the opening of the cave. "Nestor!" he exclaimed, relieved to see the old caretaker alive and well. He moved to untie Nestor from the rope that bound his wrists.

They saw Leonard with a rag in his hand, holding it over the nose of Diego. Leonard then quickly tied the hands of the two thieves, who appeared to be knocked unconscious. Leonard towered over them, a scowl on his face. "Come on, lad," he barked. "Leave that silly old man alone. Come lend a hand with these two sleeping beauties. We have to work fast before they wake up again."

Jason gagged the unfortunate thieves. "What did you do?" he asked Leonard.

Leonard grinned. "Camphor," he said, holding up the rag. "Puts them to sleep, that's all. They'll be fine. Well, they'll wake up with tremendous head-aches, but they'll be fine . . . eventually."

During this entire operation, Nestor stayed out of

the way, leaving Leonard to decide what to do and how to do it.

"Get on the cart and take the reins," Leonard told Nestor. "The boy and I will load these two on the back. I'll walk along beside you."

"What's the plan now?" Jason asked after the cargo was loaded. He eagerly climbed aboard the cart to sit beside Nestor.

"Back to Argo Manor," Leonard answered. "We have to take them back where they came from, and fast. Isn't that right, Nestor?"

Nestor grunted in agreement.

They traveled in silence for some time.

"What would have happened if we failed?" Jason asked. "What if we couldn't have gotten them back? Would Rick and Julia have been trapped in Venice forever?"

"Perhaps," Nestor said.

"Would the Door to Time have been closed forever?" Jason probed.

"Oh, don't ask Nestor, lad," Leonard blurted. "He won't tell you the truth. It's not so simple to keep that door closed! Aren't I right, friend?"

Nestor stared appraisingly at Leonard. "It is not so easy to open, either," Nestor said curtly, as if to remind Leonard of something that happened a long time ago.

"What's with you two guys?" Jason asked. "I can't tell whether you're friends or enemies."

Leonard looked away. Nestor scowled. "The four keys always return," he said. "One way or the other, the keys always find their way back."

"I don't understand," Jason said.

"Somebody in Kilmore Cove receives a package in the mail — a package containing the four keys," Nestor continued. "And everything begins all over again."

"That's what happened to us two days ago!" Jason said. "We found a mail receipt and picked up a package. That's how we got the keys."

"That is how it always begins," Leonard joined in. "But who sends the packages? That's the question, lad, the question without an answer." He spat on the ground. "It is a mystery that can never be unraveled. Isn't that right, Nestor?"

Nestor gave no answer.

Leonard touched Jason's elbow. "Do you know what Ulysses used to say about your friend, Nestor the gardener?"

"Leonard, that's enough!" Nestor ordered.

Leonard smiled broadly, then tipped his head in deference. "My lips are sealed," he said, chuckling softly.

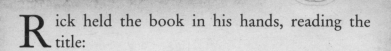

R ick held the book in his hands, reading the title:

Encyclopedie ou Dictionnaire Raisonné des Sciences, des Arts, et des Metiers

So the mysterious object that Signor Caller had kept hidden was an ordinary book. But what left Rick speechless was not the book itself but rather, the type with which it was printed. The letter *d* particularly stuck out, raised a smidgen above the other letters, a flying *d*. It was identical to the flying *d* stamped on the documents that he had in his pocket, the ones the Old Owl of Kilmore Cove had spit out. None other than Peter Dedalus himself, as Rick knew all too well, had invented the Old Owl. Holding the book in his hands, Rick knew that he had a valuable clue, a clue that connected this book, and in turn, the Callers, to Peter Dedalus.

"Here they come," Julia whispered. "Quick, put it away." She rose to stand in front of Rick, waving to the Callers, but also obscuring the book from their view.

"You must excuse us," Alberto said, glancing at Rosella. "We had some unpleasant business that demanded our attention."

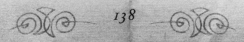

"Who was that man with the weird mask?" Julia asked.

"They call him Count Ashes," Alberto replied. "He's a member of the secret guards."

"Some secret," Julia scoffed. "You sure recognized him quickly."

"We recognize the mask that he wears," Rosella said. "But we don't know who hides beneath it."

"What does he want with you?" Rick asked.

"It is none of your concern," Alberto said stiffly. "Come, we have to continue looking for your friend, Peter."

Rick paused, then said, "I think I found another way of finding him."

"Oh?" Rosella asked.

"The book that you're hiding," Rick said. "I believe it was printed by him."

Alberto's face went pale. He looked around furtively, making sure that no one had overheard.

"I had to look inside," Rick said in apology. "I needed to know what we were hiding."

"Yes, yes, we understand," Rosella said, nodding seriously.

"I just didn't want it to be drugs or anything like that," Rick said. "When we saw that it was only a book, we felt so relieved."

"Only a book," Alberto echoed. "But still something very illegal. We live in dangerous times."

"Tell them about the flying *d*," Julia urged Rick.

He explained to the Callers about the unique typesetting of the book. "They're exactly the same!" he said, showing them the papers that he carried in his pocket — the papers that he had retrieved just that morning in Kilmore Cove, more than two hundred years in the future. "It's the same typesetting," Rick said. "It's Peter's signature."

"Where did you get those papers?" Alberto asked.

"From Kilmore Cove, in England," Rick answered. "Like I told you, they were printed by a printing press invented by Peter Dedalus."

"Oh my Lord, Alberto!" Rosella said, examining the documents. "The boy is right."

"If you can tell us where your book was printed, it might bring us a step closer to Peter," Julia said.

Alberto lifted the cloth to uncover the hidden book. He opened it and leafed through the pages, which smelled of paper and fresh ink. "It's not so simple," Alberto said with a sigh. "You see, I printed this book myself."

"What?" Rick gasped.

"Come," Alberto said. "I will show you, but we must take care that we are not followed."

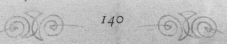

They followed Alberto through a dizzying array of back alleys, narrow roads, and crowded markets. Finally, as they walked down a side road, which seemed abandoned, Alberto stopped. "Be careful not to slip," he warned them, leading them down a stairway to a canal.

They walked in a few inches of water on a stone floor that was slimy with algae.

"Since the secret guards began to watch the city," whispered Alberto, "we typesetters had to go into hiding. We're almost there."

The pavement began to slope upward slowly, eventually becoming dry. A hallway led to . . . a dead end. Rosella made a sign for the puzzled children to remain quiet while Alberto checked that they were, in fact, completely alone and unseen.

He inserted a large key into a well-hidden keyhole, turned it, and opened a hidden door that was cleverly concealed in the stone. Alberto led his guests into a small, cluttered room. "Welcome to my secret printing house!"

"Wow! That's like, sooo cool," Julia said.

Alberto lit the oil lamps on the walls. The room had several large black machines covered with sheets of paper. All over the room there were pages hanging on a rope to dry. On the floor there were rolls of paper, inkwells, and wooden shavings. The table was littered with rulers, squares, paper cutters, and rectangular matrixes on which pages of books were set. The air had a distinctive aroma of glue.

"We're just a short distance from our house," Rosella said.

"This printing press was sold to me along with Penelope's house," Alberto informed them.

He showed Rick and Julia the cabinet that contained all kinds of loose metal letters. The capital letters and lowercase letters were carved into rectangular pieces of metal. When a book or paper was to be printed, each letter was set by hand, one after another, to form all the words that were to be printed on every page.

Alberto searched for the drawer that contained the letter *d*s and took out a pair. "These are the letters," he said. Albert lowered the metal letter into a stamp pad soaked with ink and laid it on a white sheet of paper. The letter *d* came out perfectly, without any flaw.

"It's not the *d* we're looking for," Julia noted.

"You are correct," Alberto said. "The flying *d* is due to an imperfection in the press itself. Do you see that machine there? After I make up a page with these letters, I carefully insert the entire frame. Then

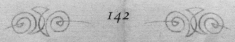

I pull that lever. The press soaks the letters with ink, lets a sheet of paper roll through, and prints the words on the paper by applying pressure from above." He looked searchingly at Julia and Rick. "Understand?"

"Sort of," Julia answered, "in a 'not really' kind of way."

Alberto continued, "When the page comes out, for some reason all the *d*s change to those you have seen printed on the encyclopedia and on your papers."

"A flying *d*," Julia commented.

"Peter's signature," Rick added.

"Some collectors have already noticed that," continued Alberto. "My editions are considered unique and are, therefore, very much in demand. But it's not easy to print anything while trying to evade the secret guards that hound me."

"I don't understand," Julia said. "Why do you need to hide?"

"Until a short time ago," Alberto said, "Venice boasted some of the best printers in the world. However, certain types of books drew criticism."

"Books on magic were prohibited," Rosella said, by way of clarification. "The Council of Ten used that law to control the activity of the various typographers. They wanted to control what was being printed."

"Yes," Alberto said, "they want to control ideas, for they know and fear the power of the word."

"But your book is just an encyclopedia," Julia said. "How can that be prohibited?"

Alberto simply shook his head. "For some people in power, even facts are frightening. New ideas can lead to change. There are forces in our society that want things to remain the same. They are afraid of the truth."

Rick moved closer to the press. He recognized Peter's handiwork on some of the details: the dental wheels of various dimensions, the use of gears and wooden supports. It was definitely his work. Peter had been here when Penelope lived in Venice . . . when he was still Ulysses Moore's friend.

Rick pulled out the page he had gotten from the Old Owl. He read it over and over again.

"What are you thinking, Rick?" Julia asked, snapping Rick out of his reverie.

He said almost to himself, "To find Peter, we need to use the correct key and write DEDA."

"You already tried that in Kilmore Cove," Julia reminded him.

"I guess I didn't type the right key," Rick

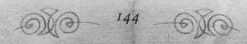

responded. "Maybe it's the key that Oblivia has, the key she used to open the Door to Time in the House of Mirrors."

"I have a suggestion," Alberto offered. "You could try printing DEDA on this machine. Perhaps your friend left a clue that can help you find him."

Alberto tied on an apron, took an empty matrix frame, and aligned four letters: DEDA. He inserted the matrix in the press and pulled a lever. He waited for something to happen. The machine puffed, and with a jerk, it grabbed the matrix, dipped it in ink, and spit out a white page on the opposite side: DEDA. He took the wet sheet and showed it to the others.

"Nothing happened," he said, frowning.

Rick examined the sheet with disappointment. "I wish Jason were here," he said, thinking of how his friend had helped solve riddles before.

Julia spoke up. "I think that Peter wanted to be found by his friends; he wanted to be forgiven. Do you remember what was said in the confession that he left behind?" she asked. "He ran away because he was ashamed. He didn't have the courage to admit the secrets he foolishly revealed to Oblivia."

"Hmmmm, you could be right," Rick agreed.

"Well, neither Ulysses nor Penelope ever found that record. We found it. Nobody else could have known what had happened to him, or exactly why he ran away. After opening the door, he mailed the lion key to Ulysses."

Rosella shook her head, amazed. "What a bizarre story!"

"In reality, he wanted to be found," Julia persisted. "Otherwise, why would he have hidden the record in the chessboard? He purposely made the wrong move to force Ulysses to checkmate him. By forcing a checkmate the secret drawer would open. Don't you see, Rick? Even though Peter ran away, ashamed, there's a part of him that is aching to be found."

"Okay, let's say you're right," Rick countered. "Suppose he wanted Ulysses to follow him. Maybe, just maybe, he left other clues."

Julia slapped her forehead and exclaimed, "Of course! Remember the map in the notebook? We need to find the Calle Love of Friends!"

Rick turned to Alberto and Rosella. "Have you ever heard of it?"

They shook their heads no.

Rick sighed. "We're right back where we started."

"I simply can't believe that Ulysses' manuscript is of no use at all!" insisted Julia. "He knew where all

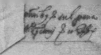

the doors emerged." She opened the journal and flipped the pages.

"Don't forget the music box and the frame!" Rosella reminded them. "We still need to talk with whoever made them," she said, lifting the painting that she had been carrying for half of the day.

Rick was too absorbed in studying the sheet that had just been printed. He murmured to himself, "Use the right key and write DEDA. The right key . . ."

Some fruitless moments passed without a word. Rick felt unbelievably frustrated. "I'm missing something obvious," he said. "There's a clue right before my eyes, but I can't see it."

Alberto coughed. "Perhaps, ahem, a rest is in order. Let's conclude our search for today," he suggested. "We can return home, eat a nice dinner and . . ."

Still struggling for the answer, Rick ignored Alberto. He was not one to give up easily. "There's got to be a solution," he said, as if trying to convince himself. He paced the floor like a tiger in a cage. "What if DEDA isn't a word at all?"

"If it's not a word, what else could it be?" Julia asked.

"Peter wrote that the right key is not the lower one, so it must be the upper one."

"Maybe it's on top of the machine?" guessed Alberto.

"Upper key . . . upper key . . ." whispered Rosella, taking part in the hunt.

"It's not a word, it's not a number," Rick repeated. Suddenly he stopped in the middle of the room. Nestor's words popped into his head. "Music! Peter loved music!" Rick exclaimed. "What if the right key . . . is a musical note?"

"They don't look to me like musical notes," Alberto said. "Musical notes are usually written on a staff sheet."

"A sharp key — not a flat key!" Rosella chimed in.

Rick clapped his hands together. "That's it! That's the key!"

Alberto looked at the sheet, still perplexed. "If you'd like, I have all of the musical notes. The only problem is that the sheet is written *deda*, not do, re, mi, fa, sol, la . . ."

"Because that's the way we write notes in England!" Rick explained. "We use letters. Do is written as a *C*, re as a *D*, mi as an *E*, and the *A* is la."

Alberto worked at the printing machine. He said to Rick, "Hmmmm, according to your theory, we should insert the re, mi, re, la, in a music sheet . . . in treble clef?" he asked.

Rick shrugged. "I'm not sure of anything. We've got to at least try."

Alberto chose the matrix suited to print music books, then aligned the metal blocks with the illustration of the staff and the treble clef. They printed the first page and, successively, loaded the symbols of the four notes in the matrix, which according to Rick's theory formed the word DEDA. They again inserted the sheet that had just come out of the printing press.

"Let's keep our fingers crossed," Julia whispered, as Alberto lowered the lever.

The page was swallowed up; the matrix was immersed in ink and pressed onto the sheet. The sheet was expelled from the opposite side with the four musical notes printed in their place on the music sheet.

Nothing happened.

Rick's shoulders sagged. Suddenly he looked exhausted, defeated.

Alberto was about to recover the sheet from the roll that had expelled it, when it began to turn itself in the opposite direction, pushing the sheet under the printing press once again. "What's happening?" he cried. "My heavens! The press is operating on its own!"

Everyone gathered around the machine, looking on in amazement. Gears and notches that had been rusted by time began to function without being cranked, making the same clicking noise as a large typewriter.

There was another ink impression, and finally the page was spit out. Alberto pulled the sheet to show the others. "Look! I'd say the song is finished!"

After the first four notes, there now came a succession of more musical notes, followed by lines of text.

Julia looked over Rick's shoulder and read aloud:

"Of dreams we are but simple sailors,
not captains, anchors, or vessels,
but men on board, those who
never know the route to the most beautiful ports.

"The Isle of Masks,
The Black Gondolier, resting by the lion."

- Chapter 19 -
THE MASTER CLOCKMAKER

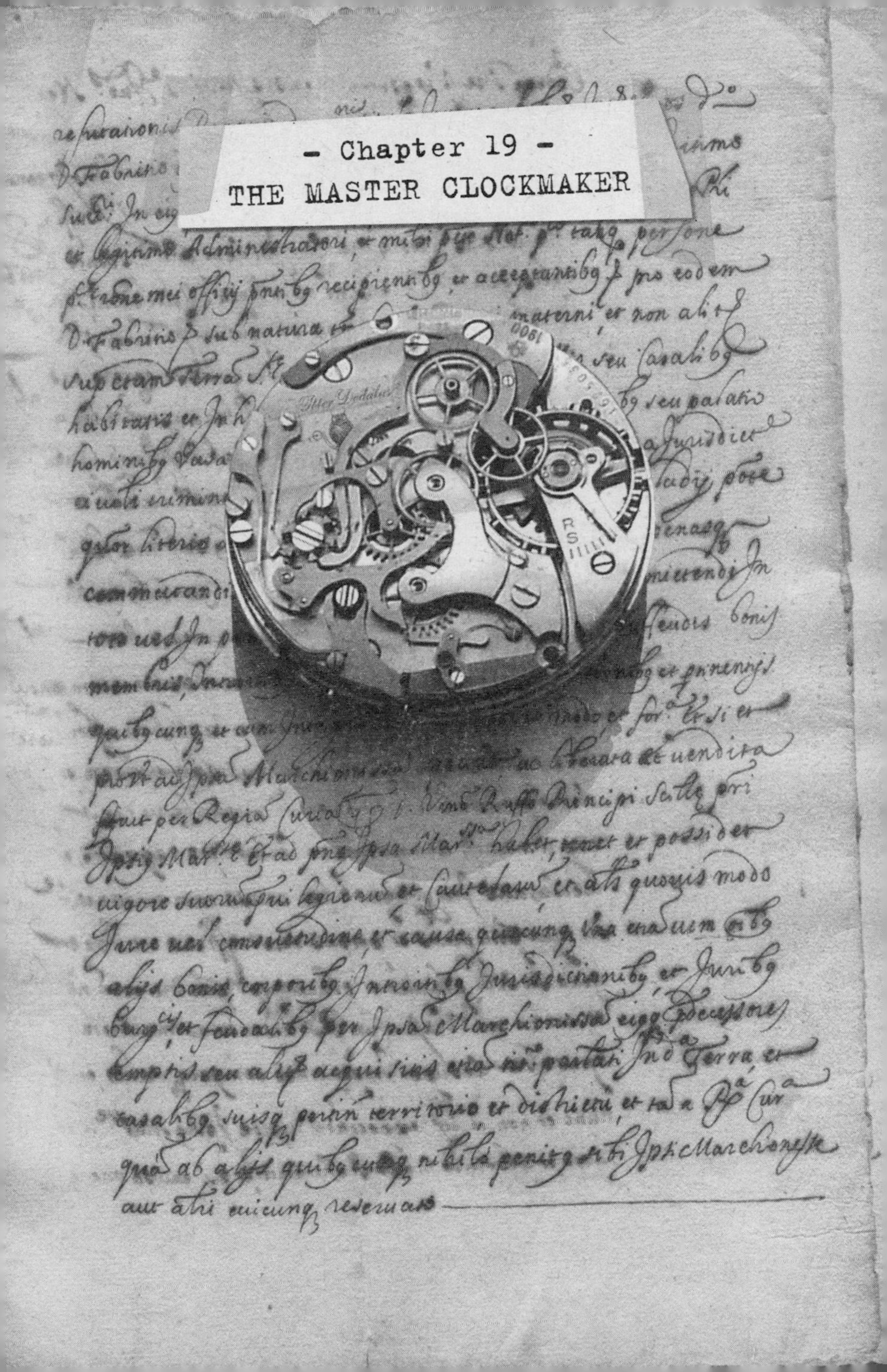

Oblivia climbed the stairs that led to the clock tower, the stairs that would lead her to Peter. She looked anxiously around but did not see anyone. Yet she heard the sharp, insistent sound of a hammer coming from above. On silent feet, Oblivia ascended the last set of stairs.

She saw a man with his back toward her and recognized him immediately. The narrow shoulders, the head topped by a tuft of unruly hair, the slight body. It could only be one man: Peter Dedalus.

"Hello, Peter," Oblivia said.

The man did not turn. He stopped hammering and held his breath.

"It's me, Peter."

The man slowly turned his head. "It's not possible," he said in a whisper.

"You have no idea how hard it was for me to find you, Peter," said Oblivia. "I've waited for this moment for a long time."

Peter Dedalus stared at a blank space on the floor. "How . . . how . . . how did you get here?" he stammered.

"From our house, Peter. I came from the House of Mirrors," Oblivia said. "I found the key and opened the door, as simple as that."

Oblivia took a step toward him; Peter stiffened

noticeably. "You're lying!" he accused. "That door has been shut for years!"

Oblivia smiled. "Things change."

"But it was closed from this side!" Peter said, trying to understand. "I even went to check on it. It was supposed to be closed forever."

"Darling," Oblivia said, her voice softening, "those doors have many secrets. Who can understand how they really work? That's why I came here to see you. I have questions; you have answers."

Peter looked about him as if to search for a way out. He stepped backward, but felt his back press against the wall.

"What did you do to them?" he asked.

"To whom, dearest?" Oblivia purred.

"Penelope and Ulysses had the map," Peter said, growing increasingly agitated. "They were the only ones who . . ."

Oblivia laughed. "Ah, the map. Well, as I said before, things change." With a sudden motion, she pulled out the map from beneath her cloak. "I'm sorry to disappoint you, dearest, but now I've got the map that shows the location of all the secret doors in Kilmore Cove."

"No, no," Peter said in disbelief. "It's impossible. You couldn't have . . ."

"Oh, Peter, please, get over it," Oblivia snapped. "Look for yourself, this is the map here in my hands! I had to go to Egypt to get it — but of course you know that, don't you, darling?"

"What did you do to Penelope and Ulysses?" Peter asked.

Oblivia put her hand on her chest in mock surprise. "I wouldn't harm a fly; surely you know that, Peter. You also know that I can be very, very kind — or have you forgotten?"

Peter blinked, swallowed hard. "I asked about Ulysses and Penelope," he demanded.

"I didn't do anything to them, Peter," Oblivia replied. "Goodness, you really do think I'm a monster, don't you? Ulysses and Penelope eliminated themselves; they threw themselves from Salton Cliff."

"No, never," Peter said in a hushed voice. "I don't believe you."

"Believe what you wish," Oblivia replied. "It is not my concern. I'm so sorry to tell this to you, Peter, but you've been away. You've missed all the excitement. Right now I'm the only friend you have left. So, my darling, come here." Oblivia opened her arms. She stepped closer. "Let me hold you."

"Those days . . . those days are gone!" Peter shouted. "It was . . . a mistake . . . a terrible mistake."

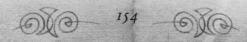

Oblivia pouted. "Didn't you miss me at all?"

"NO!"

Oblivia took another step closer. She could sense his hesitation, his weakness. "Peter, oh, Peter," she whispered. "It doesn't have to be this way."

She reached out and placed a hand on his chest. She felt him tremble. Peter stared into her eyes, then looked away. In a whisper, utterly resigned, he said, "I felt so lost and alone for so long."

"Oh, Peter," she sighed, her long fingers brushing against his cheek.

"You are so . . . so beautiful," he murmured.

"Now we can be together again," she said, her voice soft and soothing.

"I would . . . like that," he said.

"But you must trust me, darling," Oblivia said. "Share your secrets with me. Only then can we truly be happy together."

"My secrets?" Peter said. He pulled away from her. "No, no. You don't love me. You just want to use me."

"I do love you," Oblivia replied. She brought her lips close to his.

Peter pushed Oblivia out of the way, surprising her, and sent her staggering backward. Moving quickly, he raced down the stairs, fleeing her as if he were running from a monster.

Oblivia followed him down the stairs and into the street. She paused, panting, surveying Saint Mark's Square. It was packed with people. Somehow Peter Dedalus had vanished into the throng.

Oblivia stood, silently cursing, burning with anger. But at least now she knew for sure that Peter was here. She had seen the familiar weakness in his eyes, in his trembling lips.

There was only one thing to do: contact Count Ashes again. If Peter could be found once, he could surely be found once more. And next time, he wouldn't get away so easily.

Nestor drove the cart back to Argo Manor. Jason sat at his side. Leonard Minaxo walked behind, keeping an eye on the cart's unique cargo — two sleeping travelers from Venice.

Jason cast a worried look back at the cart. "Are you sure they'll be okay?" he asked Leonard.

"They'll be fine, lad, no worries," the lighthouse keeper replied.

"How long will they sleep?" Jason asked.

Leonard shrugged. "Long enough, I figure, if we hurry."

It had been decided: Leonard Minaxo would return with Jason to Venice. At first Jason protested, but there was no other way. He couldn't handle the two intruders by himself.

Jason was wary of Leonard — he did not wish to share his secret door with the lighthouse keeper. Even worse, the magical door was not Jason's secret at all, for Leonard had known about it for years.

Jason turned to Nestor. "Why didn't you tell us that Leonard knew about the ship?"

"I'm sorry, Jason," Nestor said. "I swore I wouldn't tell you."

"How many others know?" Jason asked.

"No one else, Jason," Nestor said. "I swear. Only Rick, Julia, you, me, and Leonard."

Jason felt tired and frustrated. He wasn't sure if he could believe anything Nestor said anymore. The whole day, which had started with such promise, felt wasted because of two bungling thieves. Jason cursed himself for leaving open the door. As much as he wanted to blame someone else, he knew that his carelessness was the cause of all this trouble.

At the Door to Time, Leonard finished securing the two intruders to a makeshift stretcher. He had had the idea of tying the two onto an old toboggan, so that he could pull them through the tunnels. Obviously, there was no way they could be carried all that distance.

Jason took the lead.

"It looks so different," Leonard marveled. "It's been years since I've been down here."

Finally, they reached the *Metis*. "Ah, my ship," Leonard whispered, awe and affection in his voice.

Leonard stood on the pier, admiring the great ship. He boarded and, together with Jason, tied the gagged Diego and Esme to the ship's great mast so they would not tumble from the ship during their voyage.

"Pull up the anchor," Leonard barked.

Jason paused, resentment burning inside him. Jason had been the ship's captain. But now with

Leonard around, Jason was demoted to first mate. Still, he did not complain. He just followed orders.

"Are you sure you know where we're going?" Jason called to Leonard.

The man looked to the far shore, eyes twinkling. The wind began to stir. The water swelled. The *Metis'* bow heaved. Jason glanced back at Leonard. The man stood tall at the stern, erect and powerful, at home on the water.

When the wind grew stronger in intensity, there came a booming blast.

They had crossed the time barrier.

- Chapter 21 -
REUNION

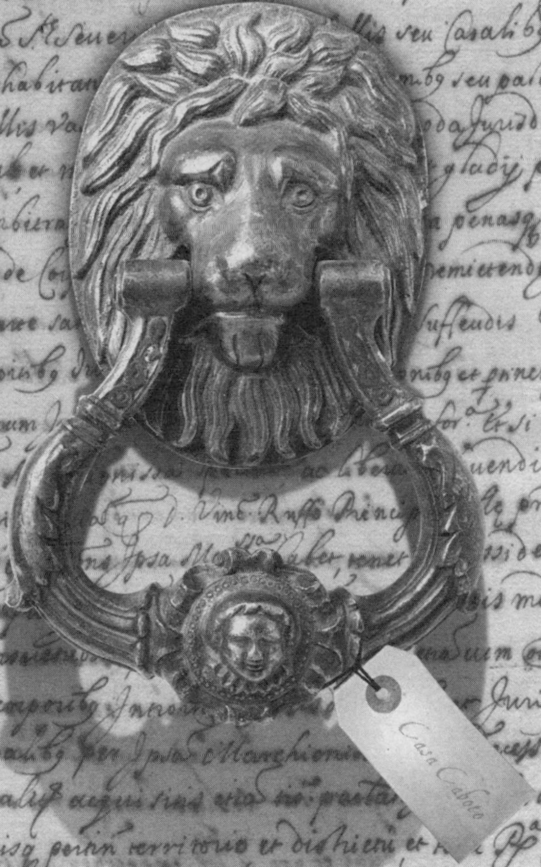

Julia and Rick sat waiting in the courtyard.

Julia stared at the closed door. "What if he doesn't come back?" she asked Rick.

"He'll be back," Rick answered.

"But what if he doesn't?" she insisted.

"He will," Rick said, smiling. "Look."

The door had opened. First Jason stepped forth, followed by a man dragging a sled of some kind. The two street urchins were on it — tied, gagged, and blindfolded.

Julia rushed into her brother's arms. After a long moment, Jason gestured to the man beside them. "This is Leonard," he explained.

"Hi," Julia said, looking back at her twin with uncertainty. "He knows?"

Jason nodded. "One of Nestor's secrets."

Leonard looked at Rick. To the surprise of the twins, he nodded and said, "You must be Banner. I met you once, long ago. You have the same hair as your father."

There was little time to waste. Julia and Rick explained that outside on the street there were a man and a woman who had helped them. The Callers, as Julia explained, were waiting to take them to the Black Gondolier. "We think we've found Peter," she said, triumph in her voice.

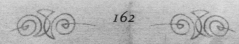

Leonard opted to stay behind. "I will tend to these two," he said, referring to Diego and Esme. "I'll make sure they recover nicely. I'll see to it that they are safe."

"Meanwhile," Julia said, "we've got to take a ride in a gondola!"

The group of five — the Callers, three kids, and the tiny dog — were excited. Julia, in particular, had a bounce in her step and a smile a mile wide.

"Alberto and Rosella have been phenomenal, Jason!" Julia chirped. "They've been a huge help."

"Oh please, don't exaggerate," Alberto said. "After all, it wasn't so hard to find this Black Gondolier."

"Black Gondolier?" Jason asked.

"Peter doesn't live in Venice," Julia explained. "We believe he lives on a nearby island called the Isle of Masks. We are supposed to meet with the Black Gondolier at dusk and he'll take us there."

"Where do we meet him?" Jason asked.

"It was a brain-buster of a riddle," Julia replied. "Without Alberto, we might not have ever figured it out! On the sheet it said, *at the lion's resting place.*"

Jason thought for about two seconds. He loved riddles, and had an uncanny knack for solving them. "Hmmmm, I once read something like that in a magazine." He mused, and then added, "Is there a statue of a lion anywhere around here? 'At the lion's resting place' could mean his shadow."

Rosella laughed out loud, amazed at Jason's intuition. "That's it!" she exclaimed. "Unfortunately, it took all of us twenty agonizing minutes to figure it out!"

Rick nodded at Jason. "You see, we really did miss you, buddy."

"Alberto is convinced that the Black Gondolier will be at the very point where the lion statue's shadow falls," Julia continued.

"And where is the statue?" Rick asked.

"There," Alberto said, pointing to a distant spot. "Five minutes away."

The day was nearing its end, and the setting sun washed over the roofs of Venice with burnished browns and golds.

Jason felt a wild new hope surge in his heart. Peter Dedalus was alive — and they were on their way to see him! It was unbelievable. For here he was, walking the streets of Venice, a mangy dog named Fleabag nipping at his heels. What an amazing adventure!

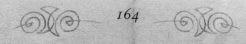

Now they needed to find the Black Gondolier, supposedly the only person who could navigate through the labyrinthine canals of the city to take them to the Isle of Masks.

"I'm worried about Oblivia Newton," Julia said.

Rick looked at her, puzzled. "Why? She's back at Kilmore Cove."

"She found you in Egypt," Julia noted. "She knows how to travel through time."

Rick slid his eyes toward Jason, who returned his apprehensive gaze. Julia was right. Oblivia Newton always found a way to mess up their plans. Rick stared at the long shadow that fell across the lagoon from the statue. "At the lion's resting place," he murmured.

There it was: a gondola, lazing in the water. Inside of it, a massive black man with a red silk turban covering his head lay with his eyes closed. He appeared to be asleep.

They had found the Black Gondolier.

"Where do you want to go?" the gondolier asked, after being roused from his sleep.

"To the Isle of Masks," Alberto answered.

The man sneered. "It doesn't exist."

"Our friend told us that you, of all the people in Venice, would be the one who could guide us there," Alberto persisted.

The gondolier stretched his strong arms and yawned. "Who would your friend be?" he asked.

"Peter Dedalus," Alberto replied.

The gondolier shook his head. "Don't know who that is," he said.

"Maybe he changed his name," Julia spoke up. "After all, he is hiding."

The gondolier raised an eyebrow. "Hiding? Is your friend in trouble? I won't be a part of anything illegal," he declared.

"No, no, I assure you," Alberto said, "nothing illegal at all. Sir," he said, "we merely wish to visit the Isle of Masks. Look at us. Do we look like criminals? We were told that you were the only man who could take us there. Please, sir. You shall be well paid for your time."

The gondolier sat thoughtfully, rubbing his chin with a rough hand. "Perhaps your friend's name is Peter Englishman?" he asked.

Jason smiled. "Yes! That's him, I'm sure of it!" he said without hesitation.

"Then hand me five gold coins and climb aboard!" the gondolier said. "Let's take a ride."

The gondola glided effortlessly through the smooth water, quickly leaving the city behind. At sunset, the flat water seemed ablaze with fire, the water reflecting the sunset. The sandy shoals were crowded by wading birds, while eels swam in swirling coils under the water's surface.

"The lantern," ordered the gondolier as darkness fell around them. He rowed steadily into the fog, which closed around them like a wall. Blanketed in gray, they went farther into the water, forced to trust the gondolier's sense of direction. All around, they could see only darkness and fog. Finally, the bottom of the gondola scratched against a sandy shore and stopped.

"Saint George of the Algae," announced the gondolier. "The Isle of Masks."

They found themselves on a beach that gradually gave way to a wooded area. A narrow path wound itself into the interior of the island. The gondolier told the travelers to follow it.

"The few homes on this island are all on the eastern side," explained the gondolier. "On the western side, there's an old monastery. Peter Englishman lives with the old monks in a wooden house behind its stone walls."

"How far is it?" Rick asked.

"Fifteen minutes," the gondolier answered. "If you don't get lost."

"What?" Julia said, alarmed.

The man laughed. "Just stay on the path and don't mind the snakes."

"Snakes?" Julia repeated.

The gondolier laughed again. "No worries," he said, "most of them aren't poisonous!"

"Most?" Julia said. She turned to Rick. "Did he say, *most*?"

"Rosella and I will wait here," Alberto told Rick and the others. "This is your business, not ours."

Rick looked to Jason, who nodded in agreement.

Rosella squeezed Julia's hand as if to warn her to be careful. The girl took the dog in her arms. In moments, they vanished into the woods behind the two boys.

The gondolier busied himself by pulling his craft onto the shore. Once again, he stretched his long body into the boat, folded his arms behind his head, and closed his eyes.

Rosella and Alberto stood close together, hand in hand. A sharp noise came from the nearby woods, the sound of a branch breaking. It startled Rosella. "Alberto, did you hear it? What was that?" asked Rosella, scrutinizing the fog.

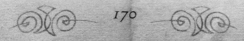

"Okay," Julia said as they walked the dark path, "this place officially creeps me out."

Rick laughed. "So it's official, huh?"

"Look," Jason said, pointing. "That must be the outside wall that circles the monastery."

Beyond the wall, they could discern the low, square construction of the monastery. Here the path climbed a slight hill, affording the three friends a better view of the complex. There was a small church with a modest bell tower. They glimpsed the guttering flames of candles through the windows of the church.

"Listen," Jason said. He held up a hand for silence.

Rick and Julia soon heard it: the low chant of male voices.

"What are they saying?" Julia wondered.

Rick shook his head. "Some kind of prayer, I guess. It's in Latin, I think."

Peering through the fog, Jason saw what he guessed was Peter's house. It was a simple wooden structure, nestled between the wall and the back of the church. The windows were lit. It looked like Peter was home — and awake.

They drew nearer, then came to a halt. A woman's voice echoed from inside the dwelling.

"It's her, isn't it?" Julia said.

Rick nodded. He, too, recognized the voice. It was Oblivia Newton.

"Let's get closer," Jason suggested. "I want to hear what they're saying."

Hidden by the underbrush, Count Ashes took off his mask. He breathed the fresh night air in deeply. He placed a hand in his pocket and felt the heavy coins. Now all he had to do was wait for Oblivia to run her errand, return the woman to Venice, and his work would be done. A very nice payday for a simple task — finding a clockmaker, easy work!

To pass the time, the count decided to explore the island; he had never set foot on it before. But while walking on the path, he heard voices and instinctively sought cover. He watched as three children walked toward the monastery. *Hmmmm, very odd,* he thought. His curiosity roused, the count followed the path back toward the shore. He soon noticed the pale yellow light of the gondola's lantern. Drawing closer, he noted two shadows standing close together, hand in hand. That's when he accidentally snapped a small branch.

"Alberto, did you hear it? What was that?" said a woman's voice. The count immediately recognized the voice. It was Rosella Caller! She sounded frightened, and this pleased the count.

The count crouched low, listening intently. A thousand questions raced in his mind. Why were they here? What were they up to?

"I hope the children are not long," commented Rosella.

"You heard the gondolier," Alberto said, in an attempt to reassure his wife. "The clockmaker's house is not far."

Again, the clockmaker! What was so important about that man? wondered Count Ashes.

At once, he made his decision. It was time to take a look into the mysterious Peter Englishman. Silently, on stealthy feet, the count rose and hurried back up the path. Unseen and unheard, he strode in the direction of the monastery.

- Chapter 23 -
THE MEETING

By climbing onto the rear wall of the monastery, Rick and Jason were able to get into Peter's house through an open second-story window. After instructing Fleabag to "hush," Julia followed suit — shimmying through the window. She entered a darkened room that appeared to be some sort of workshop filled with incomprehensible mechanical oddities. At one end of the room, a staircase descended to the floor below. She saw Jason and Rick stealthily moving toward the head of the stairs, crouching low and stepping softly. Voices filtered up the steps. Two voices, in fact: a man's and a woman's.

Oblivia and Peter, no doubt.

Flat on his belly, Jason peered down into the room below. It was the first time he had ever seen Peter Dedalus. The man was quite small — frail, really, as if he might suddenly break. Peter wore glasses perched on a long, rodent-like nose.

"Why won't you leave me alone?" he moaned.

"Peter, my darling," Oblivia said in soothing tones.

"Don't call me darling! I'm fully aware you don't care about me!" Peter said. "I know that you've always deceived me. And here you are again, still trying to deceive me. But I won't let you do it, Oblivia, not ever again."

"Oh, Peter," Oblivia protested. "You are wrong about me."

"You only want to know about the doors," he said, his voice rising in accusation. "That's all you've ever cared about: the doors, the keys, the secrets."

Oblivia sat down. She calmly sipped a glass of wine and observed Peter with cool precision. "Peter, look at me. I am here with you, alone in your house. Just the two of us. It can be like it used to be between us," she said. "You don't have to be alone anymore."

"I don't believe you," Peter replied. "You just want the keys."

"Wake up, Peter," Oblivia said, her voice turning icy. "I already know what you did. You and your friends tried to hide all the doors. You took all the keys out of circulation. And it worked, for a while."

Oblivia reached to her neck and pulled out a necklace that had been obscured beneath her blouse. A Cat Key and Lion Key dangled from the chain.

"The Lion Key!" Peter exclaimed. "You can't possibly have it, Oblivia!"

Oblivia shrugged, smiling. "It's our key, Peter. The key that opens the door that you made."

"No!" he cried. "You've got everything wrong. I did not make any doors! The door was already there. . . . All the doors already existed."

Oblivia leaned forward. "Who made the doors, Peter?"

"No one knows!" the little man replied. "Not even Ulysses or Penelope. No one knows — and no one will ever know. It was one of our rules."

"Rules, Peter?"

He backed into a corner of the room, holding his head between his hands. "Yes, rules," he whispered. "Rules that I broke. Friendships that I betrayed."

Oblivia casually folded her legs. She seemed almost to be enjoying Peter's agony. "Let's talk more about the rules, Peter."

"No . . . please, no more . . . I can't do this," he said, as if asking for mercy.

"Oh, Peter, can't you see? Your old friends are gone," she said. "I'm the only one left. The secret can be ours to share, our adventure . . . together."

Peter stood with his arms wrapped around himself, oddly bent to one side. "How did you get the keys?" he asked. "I opened the door to the House of

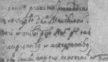

Mirrors. I took the key and mailed it to Ulysses. He was supposed to keep it safe."

"It is safe," Oblivia answered. "Safe with me, while Ulysses is buried six feet under the ground. The caretaker had the key . . . for a while, anyway."

"The caretaker?" Peter asked, incredulous.

"Yes, the old gardener," confirmed Oblivia. "Nestor."

"Nestor," Peter repeated, the faintest of smiles on his face. "That crazy old man . . ." Peter looked at her attentively. "Maybe he was the one who reopened it with the Master Key."

"Very good, Peter," Oblivia said, smiling warmly. "This is news to me. What Master Key?"

"I cannot tell you, Oblivia," he quickly replied. "I made a promise. It's against the rules!"

"What rules are you talking about, Peter?" Oblivia snapped back. "It's just you and I, Peter. There are no rules between us!"

Peter took a deep breath. He said, "First rule: Protect Kilmore Cove. Second rule: Do not talk about the doors with anyone. Third rule: Do not try to discover who made them."

Oblivia paused a moment, then laughed softly. "Oh my goodness, Peter, you are such a little Boy

Scout. I'm dying to know who made up these silly rules. Please, Peter, satisfy my curiosity."

"Moore," he answered.

"Ah, Ulysses Moore," she purred. "What is it that they say about dead men? Oh yes, dead men tell no secrets." Oblivia stood up and gently placed her wineglass on the table. She walked toward Peter. "Tell me, Peter. Whisper it softly in my ear. Tell me about the Master Key."

Bark, bark, bark. A small dog barked outside the window, as if warning of an intruder.

"I'll check it out," Jason whispered. He quietly crossed the room, careful not to make a sound, and lowered himself out the window and onto the surrounding wall. By the time he touched the ground, the dog had stopped barking.

"Fleabag," Jason called into the night. "Here, doggie, doggie." He headed toward the direction of the woods. Then he saw the dog, lying in a heap on the path. He wasn't moving.

"Fleabag?"

The boy slowly approached the dark shape, hoping that his eyes had deceived him. Suddenly, a gloved hand grabbed Jason from behind, yanking

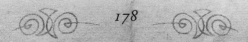

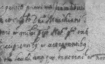

hard on his neck. A tall figure, wearing the grotesque mask of a bird, appeared in front of him.

"Not a sound, you little piece of filth, or I'll give you the same as your little dog," warned Count Ashes.

Oblivia looked out the window, alarmed by the dog's barking. After it stopped, she turned back to Peter.

She tried a new approach. "Perhaps I haven't been, um, understanding enough," she admitted. "Perhaps, Peter, if you explained it to me, if you *helped* me understand, then maybe we could reach an agreement."

Peter looked into her eyes. How he wanted to believe her. He began, "Kilmore Cove was at risk of becoming an amusement town, like a Disney theme park where one only needed a ticket for the ride of a lifetime," he said.

"I love Disney," Oblivia said. "People go there to spend millions of dollars every year."

"We felt otherwise," Peter said sharply.

"So instead of sharing this secret — this gift, this wonder of wonders — you and your little group decided to try to hide the doors for all time," Oblivia said, scorn in her voice. "That's insanity. Can't you see that? This is the twenty-first century, Peter. This is the age of the Internet, satellites, and cell phones. We're in a world of mass communication and cyberspace. And you . . . and your friends . . . want to crawl under a rock!"

"No, that's not the way it was," Peter protested. "We didn't want Kilmore Cove to become over-run with commercialism. Our beautiful little village would have been turned into a giant gift shop, complete with tacky hotels and tourists. It was our mission to protect Kilmore Cove. We would have even denied ourselves the joy of traveling through time as long as we could have achieved it."

Oblivia smiled tightly. "That's when I entered the story, isn't it, Peter?"

"I loved you," Peter said, his voice faint and resigned.

"And I loved you," Oblivia replied. "But one day you ran off without even saying good-bye. Think of how that made me feel."

"You didn't love me, Oblivia," Peter replied. "You only wished to control all the doors. I under-stand that now."

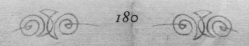

Oblivia shrugged and for the first time gave Peter an honest smile. "Actually, I still want that. I won't deny it, Peter. Make it your parting gift to me. One final gift and I will get out of your life forever — if that's what you wish. Please, darling, don't make me get down on my knees . . . and beg," Oblivia said. She was close to him now, her fingers in his hair.

Peter stood frozen, bewitched by Oblivia's charms. He had been lonely for so long. "Wait," he managed to whisper. He walked to a cabinet and opened a drawer. He took out an old scrapbook filled with photographs. "I have missed Kilmore Cove," he confessed. "I longed to see the people I knew. Even you, Oblivia; I missed you, too. In these last few years I have thought of nothing else. I sat and looked at those old photos night after night, yearning to return to Kilmore Cove, yet too frightened to face the consequences."

Oblivia distractedly opened the album.

"I even tried to go back," Peter continued. "I went to the Calle Love of Friends to see if the door was still open. But it was closed. I figured that someone had gone through the door in my place and emerged in Kilmore Cove."

"Interesting," Oblivia clucked. "Someone took your place?"

Peter shook his head. "I don't know for sure."

Oblivia lingered over a photograph. There was something about it. "Who is this person with you by the lighthouse?" she asked.

"That's Ulysses," Peter replied, sitting down beside her.

"So that's the famous Ulysses Moore," Oblivia said. She stared at the photo attentively. "How old is this picture?"

"Twenty years, at least," Peter answered.

"I'm sorry, I interrupted your story," Oblivia said. She placed a hand on Peter's knee. "What did you do after you found that the door was closed?"

"I convinced myself that the others had been able to find the Master Key . . . and had closed the door forever," he said.

"A Master Key," Oblivia murmured.

"Yes," Peter said, excited by the topic. "A key that controls all the doors," he explained. "I analyzed all the locks, one by one. I became convinced that there was one key that could open and close every door. Then Ulysses discovered a clue about the Master Key in an old book in his library, *The Escapist's Manual*. The book deals with all kinds of keys, locks, secret passages, and devices used for escape."

"Fascinating," Oblivia purred.

"In the book, there was an essay written by Ulysses Moore's grandfather, Raymond Moore. It referred, however obliquely, to the doors. The essay even contained a drawing of the Master Key."

"How wonderful," Oblivia said. "That's exactly what I need. One key that is capable of opening all the doors in Kilmore Cove!"

"That's not the best part," Peter said with a smile. "The Master Key opens not only the doors in Kilmore Cove, but all the Doors to Time, everywhere."

He added, "The Master Key was like a pass key for the original makers of the doors."

"Who are these makers?" Oblivia asked.

"We never found out," Peter confided. "But when we decided to protect Kilmore Cove, we knew we needed to find the Master Key. We searched everywhere. If it ever truly existed, it would not only have allowed us to open all the doors, but to close them."

"Close them?" Oblivia said. The expression on her face darkened.

"When you walk through the Door to Time from Kilmore Cove," Peter explained, "it remains open until someone walks through it from the opposite

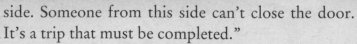

side. Someone from this side can't close the door. It's a trip that must be completed."

"I don't understand," Oblivia said.

"The Master Key can open and close the doors on either side. Whoever controls it can close all the adjoining doors forever," Peter said. "I believe that it can be used to make it so a place in time can never be reached again, preserving it and protecting it from every danger."

Oblivia imagined all the doors, all the possibilities, all the riches she could accumulate. "I want it," she said simply.

"Everybody wanted it, Oblivia. We came close to finding it, too. But then . . . I fled," Peter said. He awkwardly stood and walked across the room.

"Where is it?" she demanded.

"I have no idea. Isn't that funny, Oblivia? You want only one thing from me . . . and I have no way of giving it to you." He laughed out loud. "I'm useless to you after all."

"Did Moore ever have it?" she asked.

Peter shrugged. "I honestly can't answer that. Ulysses Moore was a man who kept his secrets."

Peter paused for a moment, struck by a thought. "What about Black? What happened to him?"

"Black?" Oblivia asked, puzzled. "Who is Black?"

"The Black Volcano," Peter said, beaming at a distant memory. "He was the train engineer. When I ran away, only three remained: Ulysses, Penelope, and Black."

"Never heard of him," Oblivia said, scowling.

Peter walked over to the photo album. "Here he is, look at him," he said. "What a presence, with his enormous beard. Black was the one who first became convinced of the existence of the Master Key."

"Black Volcano . . ." murmured Oblivia to herself. "So there's another one left after all."

She unrolled the map of Kilmore Cove on the table and asked, "Where does he live?"

"The train station," Peter answered, pointing to the map.

"There's a door at the train station!" Oblivia noted, thrilled. "A door that I'm sure you know how to open, aren't I right, Peter?"

"It requires the Horse Key," he told her, as if the information was of no consequence.

Oblivia grabbed Peter's shirt, pulled him toward her, and planted a kiss on his lips. "Bravo, Peter! You are truly wonderful! But now you must tell me where I can find the Horse Key."

The front door suddenly flew open. A man's deep voice boomed, "Before doing that, the two of you are going to tell me exactly what's going on around here. But first, allow me to extend my civilities." The masked man bowed low. "Mr. Englishman, I am glad to make your acquaintance. Ms. Newton, it's a pleasure to see you again. You may call me Count Ashes."

Then, with a sweeping gesture, Count Ashes threw Jason into the room, where he tumbled to the floor.

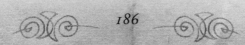

Rick and Julia gripped each other in panic. Jason was down there, possibly hurt, while they watched helplessly from the top of the stairs.

Count Ashes strode into the living room. "You will explain everything to me," he demanded. "What are these doors you speak of?"

As the count moved to step over Jason's prone body, the boy made a sudden, sweeping gesture with his leg, knocking him to the ground. As he fell, the masked man shattered an oil lamp on the floor. In a terrible moment, flames licked across the floor and climbed the wall. The fire quickly spread to the curtains, the walls, the stairway. In a matter of moments, the old wooden house was ablaze!

Oblivia ran for the safety of the front door. But as she passed, Count Ashes grabbed her leg.

She kicked frantically at the fallen man, delivering several sharp blows to his head.

"Come on," Rick said to Julia, yanking at her sleeve. "Through the window, let's go."

"But Jason's down there," Julia protested. "We can't leave him!" She turned and started down the stairs, heading into the smoke and flames. She immediately began coughing, her eyes watering from the smoke. And then she was falling, falling, as the staircase collapsed with a crash.

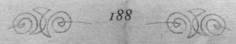

Unaware of the danger his sister faced, Jason was at Peter's side, urging him to escape. The clockmaker remained huddled in the corner, as if in a trance. "Peter, run!" Jason implored the clockmaker. "We need to get out of here now!"

Peter remained motionless. "Oblivia, my love," he murmured. "I must save her."

Jason looked over his shoulder to see Oblivia and Count Ashes locked in a deadly battle. They were surrounded by flames. "We can't get through that way!" Jason yelled. "We need to leave through this window right now! Let's go! I'm right behind you!"

Jason grabbed the clockmaker's shoulders and tried to steer him toward the first-story window, but Peter would not comply. He stared at Jason with a vacant look.

"Who are you?" Peter asked.

"A friend," Jason said. "I came from Argo Manor."

Peter looked at Jason in shock. "Argo Manor?"

"Yes, I came to find you," Jason said. He felt the heat of the fire on his skin. "There's no time to explain."

Peter suddenly seized Jason by the arms. His eyes wild, Peter said, "The Master Key is there . . . at

Argo! It has always been there," he cried. "On the tree! Find the tree!"

Peter released Jason, then plunged headlong into the fire after Oblivia.

Horrified, Jason watched as Peter became engulfed by smoke. It was impossible to see more than a few feet inside. Jason's eyes stung. He knew he couldn't last much longer.

Jason scanned a nearby table, looking for something with which to smash the window. There was a photo album, small flames licking at its pages. There was a camera! Jason grabbed it and heaved it against the window. The glass shattered. Smoke went billowing out of the house into the night air.

Without another thought, Jason grabbed what remained of the photo album and flung himself through the window.

Rick leaped down to reach Julia, who was injured from the fall. "I'll get you out, Julia, I promise," he vowed.

Rick glanced around, assessing his options. The main room was filled with smoke and flames. *No way out there.* Rick looked up at the second floor. The stairs were gone, but with a leap he knew he

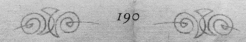

could climb up. From there, he could reach the window from which they originally entered. *But what about Julia?*

"Julia, Julia!" he cried, shaking her. "I need you to wake up!"

Julia's eyelids flickered. Then they opened wide, her eyes filled with shock and fear.

"Listen to me, Julia," Rick said. His voice was clear and surprisingly calm. He spoke with confidence. "There's a way out of here, but I need your help."

She blinked, nodding.

"Good," Rick said. "I'm going to boost you up. You have to grab hold of something and help haul yourself up to the second floor. Can you do that?"

Julia shivered once, as if snapping to attention. Yes, she nodded.

In a moment, she was up. Rick leaped high, grabbed hold, and scurried up behind her. "Through the window," he said, putting his arm around her waist. She was limping, he noticed. There was blood on her pants.

They crossed Peter's lab. The first tongues of fire had reached it. Rick kicked open the window.

"Don't worry," Rick repeated, "I'll get you out, Julia."

Rick peered out the window. Getting down would not be as easy as getting up. "Grab hold of my arm," he told Julia. Rick dropped down to the floor and lowered Julia out the window. His muscles ached; it felt as if his arm was being torn out of its socket. "Jump," he told her.

Julia looked up into his eyes.

"You can do this," he said.

She let go . . . and fell to the grass.

Rick stretched out a leg and found a foothold on the wall outside. He scampered to the ground. Then he bent low and lifted Julia in his arms. They needed to get away from the house. It could collapse any minute.

As he staggered away from the house, Rick heard the sound of breaking glass. He turned and saw someone — could it be Jason? — dive out of a first-floor window.

Rick gently set Julia down on the grass. Her face was dirty, her lip bleeding. But to Rick, at that moment, under a full moon, she looked perfect. He brushed a hand through her hair. "You're going to be all right," he assured her.

Julia smiled weakly. She reached up and found his hand, squeezed it, then closed her eyes once more.

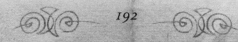

Jason saw Rick across the lawn. He was bent over his sister.

Jason ran to them, still holding the camera in his hand. The other hand held what was left of the scrapbook.

"Is she . . . ?"

Rick turned and gave Jason a quick, fierce hug. "She fell," Rick explained. "I pulled her out of the fire. I think she'll be okay."

Behind them, the house rumbled loudly, wooden beams crashing to the earth. The blaze enveloped everything that remained, red flames reaching to the sky.

"Peter?" Rick asked.

Jason looked back at the fire. He shook his head. "I don't think so," he answered. He scanned the grounds. "I don't know if any of them got out. Count Ashes, Oblivia, or Peter."

Having satisfactorily disposed of the intruders who had traveled to Argo Manor, Leonard Minaxo found himself in Venice with time to kill. The street urchins, Diego and Esme, were now dazed, confused, and far from the secret door at Cabot House. It would never open to them again.

Leonard felt unusually happy. He was back in

Venice after so many years. He enjoyed every aspect of this magnificent city — the people, art, beauty, sounds, and smells. All of it! Intending to visit the Venetian Arsenal and its shipyard, Leonard slipped through the alleyways that unraveled behind the Doge's Palace. As he walked through the streets, he was bombarded with memories of places and tales from the past. Walking amid a tumult of sensations, Leonard was surprised to find himself standing in a narrow alley before a familiar shop: Zafon Artifacts.

Leonard entered. "Ah, that aroma!" he exclaimed. "It's been such a long time since I smelled this."

A withered old man emerged from behind a mass of merchandise that had been heaped helter-skelter in a pile. He stared at Leonard, mouth agape.

"My eyes must be playing tricks on me," the dealer said. "It's either a ghost, or one of my old customers whom I haven't seen in this city for years."

"Zafon!" Leonard exclaimed, moving forward to embrace the old man. "I'm so glad to see you in good health, my old friend."

"If you keep crushing me," Zafon joked, "then I won't be in good health much longer." He stepped back to take a good look at Leonard. "What hap-

pened to you? What new seas have you traveled? What's that patch you're wearing on your eye?"

"Long story," Leonard replied, grinning mischievously.

The two old friends talked for a while, remembering old times and laughing often. When Leonard bid Zafon good-bye, promising to return soon, the old man disappeared behind a large table. He returned with two black notebooks.

"You don't want to forget your old favorites!" Zafon said. "These are the finest notebooks of the Venetian paper mills!"

Leonard held up a hand. "I can't pay for these, Zafon."

The old man waved the thought away. "It is my gift to you, for bringing happiness to an old man."

Leonard closed his large hands around the notebooks. He said, "Many thanks, Zafon. I hope to see you again soon."

The old man flashed a toothless smile. "Liar," he scolded, laughing. "You said the same thing the last time you came — and how many years ago was that?"

❈

The only thing left of Peter's house was a smoldering heap of rubble. The priests from the church had come out, and now worked to sort through the damage.

Sitting on the grass, still dazed, Julia, Rick, and Jason saw the charred body of a man carried out by several priests.

Julia gasped in fright.

"Count Ashes," Rick said.

"To think we were in there, too," Julia whispered, obviously still shaken.

Though the monks worked tirelessly amid the rubble, they found no sign of other bodies.

"Maybe they got out," Jason said. "Peter went to try to help her. You never know."

The dog, Fleabag, emerged out of the darkness, looking worn and worse than ever. Julia opened her arms to him, and the dog gave himself to her embrace.

Later, the gondolier took the Callers and the children back to Venice. It was a somber, silent journey.

Jason, for his part, could not stop thinking about Peter's last words. They echoed in his mind, over and over again: *"The Master Key is there . . . at Argo . . . it has always been there . . . on the tree . . . find the tree!"*

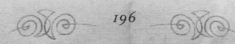

Bedraggled and weary, they finally arrived at Cabot House. "Are you sure you won't stay overnight with us?" Rosella Caller asked Rick, Jason, and Julia.

"No, Rosella. Thank you, but we really can't," Julia replied. She looked down at Fleabag, who stared up from Julia's ankles. "I was wondering if you could do me a big favor?" She picked up Fleabag and gently placed him in Rosella's arms.

"We can't take him home with us," Julia explained.

Rosella's eyes lit up. "Really! Alberto, can we?"

Alberto glanced heavenward, as if praying for deliverance. But he forced a smile to his face. He reached out a hand to pet the dog. "Of course, my love." He took out a handkerchief and vigorously wiped his hands.

"Ah, I almost forgot the painting!" Rosella exclaimed.

She handed it to Julia. "Remember the hidden music box," she noted.

"Thank you, Rosella. Thank you, Alberto," Julia said graciously. "Without you, we would never have found Peter. Even if . . ." Her voice trailed off.

"Perhaps it's for the best," Alberto said. "All things happen for a reason." He shook hands with

Rick and Jason, while bending to give Julia a delicate hug. "Today was an amazing adventure for us," he said. "Someday you'll have to come back to explain it all!"

Everyone laughed. "Sure," Jason said, "as soon as we figure it out for ourselves!"

Rick looked to his friends. "Guys," he said, "here comes Leonard. I think it's time we got home."

HOMER & HOMER
REMOVALS AND STORAGE
Helpful Staff, Packing Service, Insurance, Dismantling, Disconnecting
238 ALDERMANS HILL · PALMERS GREEN · LONDON N13 4PP

When he first saw Kilmore Cove's lights in the distance, Mr. Covenant smiled. He took a hand off the car's steering wheel and squeezed his wife's hand. "Almost home," he said.

"I miss our babies," she said. Though the twins were almost teenagers, she would forever think of them as infants, recalling the earliest days of their lives, when they were tender, pink, and helpless.

Mr. Covenant rolled down the car window. He breathed the sea air in deep. To his right, the lighthouse stood like a guardian of the town, proud and erect. "Look up on the cliff. There's Argo Manor!" Mr. Covenant exclaimed. "Home, sweet home!"

"It really is beautiful," his wife said.

"I, for one, am glad to be back," Mr. Covenant said to her. "These past few days have been a nightmare of setbacks and foul-ups," he said. "I never realized that moving could be such a headache."

"The kids will never believe what an adventure we had," Mrs. Covenant chimed in. "Broken-down trucks, lost drivers, damaged furniture — all while the children probably sat around, bored to death and missing us terribly!"

Mrs. Covenant leaned forward, peering through the windshield. "What in the world . . . ?"

Down the winding road to Argo Manor came a horse pulling a cart.

Mr. Covenant braked to a halt. "Nestor?" he said.

The caretaker nodded from his seat on the cart. "Ah, fancy meeting you here," he said.

"What are you doing with that horse?" Mr. Covenant asked.

Nestor looked at Ariadne. "Ah, well, car trouble," he mumbled. "I had to borrow her from a friend."

Mr. Covenant raised his eyebrows. He glanced at his wife and shook his head. "Must be a full moon," he murmured.

"How are the children?" called Mrs. Covenant. "Is everything all right?"

"Fine, absolutely fine," Nestor said, craning his neck to look back up the road in the direction of Argo Manor. "They are fine," he repeated, "hopefully."

"Hopefully?" croaked Mrs. Covenant.

In the courtyard of Argo Manor, Jason, Julia, and Rick stood in silence before Mr. and Mrs. Covenant. Nestor observed from a safe distance.

Mrs. Covenant paced before the trio of adventurers. They were filthy from the fire, worn and tired. Julia's pants were ripped. There was blood on her knee. Her lower lip looked swollen.

Jason was a mess. Rick didn't look much better.

Mrs. Covenant spoke first to Rick. "I'm sorry we did not get to meet under happier circumstances," she said with a scowl. "I think it's best that you return home immediately. Is that understood?"

Rick nodded, barely raising his eyes from the gravel pavement. Head hung low, he said, "Jason, Julia, I'll see you later."

Rick went to get his bicycle, stopped, and turned around, confused. "Um, has anybody seen my bicycle?"

"It's at Leonard's," Jason remembered. "You can take the Bowens' bicycle."

"Yes," Julia said, working hard not to chuckle, "the pink one."

"Leonard? The Bowens? Who *are* all these people?" wondered Mrs. Covenant.

Rick didn't stick around to answer. He hopped on the bicycle and hurried away, happy to escape Mrs. Covenant's questions.

"Now, Julia!" Mrs. Covenant said sternly. "What on earth happened to you? Are you okay?"

"It was my fault," Jason offered.

Nestor stepped forward, hoping to ease the tension. "Mrs. Covenant, I feel obligated to say that . . ."

"Not now, Nestor, please," she replied, cutting him off. "Do you see what my children look like?" She touched Jason's face, which was covered in ash, soot, and sweat.

She crossed her arms. "Well, I'm waiting. Who is going to give me an explanation?"

Jason was at a loss for words. How could he possibly explain?

"We cleaned out Dr. Bowen's cellar!" Julia suddenly exclaimed.

Jason looked at her, mouth agape. It was the first time he recalled his sister ever coming up with an excuse.

"Oh?" Mrs. Covenant said.

"He came here to ask Nestor for help," Julia continued, improvising wildly. "The three of us — me, Jason, and Rick — offered to help. I mean, there was nothing to do around here, anyway," she said as an aside. "Dr. Bowen is a really old man. The cellar . . ."

". . . was a total mess," Jason added.

"Yeah, wow, disgusting," Julia said, nodding in agreement. "*Pee-yew*, I could really use a shower."

"Anyway, we worked there for two days!" Jason said, building on Julia's story. "At the end, Dr. Bowen gave us his daughter's bicycle as a gift . . ."

". . . and this!" Julia said, holding out the painting in her hands. "It's a gift for you, Mom. Jason and I thought that you'd like it."

"For me?" Mrs. Covenant said.

"We missed you," Julia said.

"A lot," Jason added. As an afterthought he added, "You, too, Dad."

Mr. Covenant laughed softly. "That's sweet of you, Jason."

Julia pressed the painting into her mother's hands. "It's of Argo Manor," she explained.

"And there's this way cool music box that's inside the frame," Jason explained. He turned it on. In moments, Peter Dedalus' melody softly filled the garden.

"Oh my," Mrs. Covenant whispered. A small tear formed in her eye and slid down her cheek. She smiled. "It's lovely. I'd hug the both of you if you weren't so darn filthy," she said, laughing.

From a small room at the top of Argo's tower, Leonard Minaxo watched the scene in silence. He waited for the cloak of darkness to descend, for the

Covenants to enter the house, happily reunited. Then he opened the window, reached for the branch of a nearby sycamore tree, and climbed to the ground. He slipped away unseen and unheard . . . like a ghost.

- Chapter 26 -
A FINAL CLUE

Jason lay in bed, unable to sleep. His mind raced with so many thoughts. When he shut his eyes, he was back in Peter's house, surrounded by flames, coughing because of the smoke. He remembered listening while Peter and Oblivia talked.

The scene played again in his mind, like a film repeating endlessly. . . .

Oblivia had the book of photographs in her hands. She had asked, "*Who is this person with you by the lighthouse?*"

"*That's Ulysses,*" Peter had replied.

Jason still couldn't believe it. How could that be possible? How could the man in that picture — the man standing by the lighthouse — be Ulysses Moore? It didn't make any sense.

Jason climbed out of bed. He walked to the window and looked out to the sea.

The lighthouse was dark, sleeping.

Peter's camera was on the dresser, next to the few pages of the photo album that Jason had managed to salvage from the fire. Jason looked at the photos once more. One showed the clockmaker together with a short, stocky man with a thick beard.

"The Black Volcano," Jason murmured to himself.

It was the next photo that proved so troubling.

The photo of two men by the lighthouse.

Peter and . . . the other.

"*Who is this person with you by the lighthouse?*" Oblivia had asked.

"*Ulysses,*" Peter had answered.

Jason heard a noise outside the door. Footsteps.

Someone was in the hall.

The steps stopped at his door. The knob turned, the door opened.

"Julia!" Jason said, relieved.

"I can't sleep," Julia said. She sat on the edge of her brother's bed.

"Me, neither," he said.

Jason sat up at her side, still holding the photo in his hands.

Julia looked at her brother. "I don't understand," she said.

"What do you mean?" he asked.

"Peter," Julia said. "He went into the fire to save Oblivia. Do you think he loved her?"

Jason shrugged, shook his head. "I guess. I don't know," he answered.

"He knew that she was a bad person," Julia said.

Jason nodded. "Yeah, I think so. At least, he knew that she wanted the keys."

The twins sat in silence, thinking it over. Julia

sighed and said, "I think he was a lonely man. I suppose he did love her after all."

Jason thought of the fire, of Peter plunging into the flames to his almost certain death. A reckless act, yes, but also . . . truly heroic.

"Maybe we don't have a choice about who we love," Julia suggested. "Maybe the heart decides on its own."

Jason didn't answer. Honestly, he had no idea about things like love and the world of men and women. His thoughts returned to the photograph in his hands.

Julia noticed it. "What's that?" she asked.

"One of Peter's photos," Jason answered. "I saved it from the fire."

"Let me see."

It was a photograph of Peter standing beside another man in front of the lighthouse. They were both smiling.

"Julia, do you remember what Peter said?" Jason asked. "He told Oblivia that the man in this picture was Ulysses Moore."

Julia stared at the photo. "Yes, I heard it, too. He did say that," she answered in a whisper. "But . . . how could that be true?"

"I don't know," Jason said.

His eyes returned to the photograph.

The man who stood next to Peter Dedalus, smiling to the camera, was Leonard Minaxo.

Oblivia Newton slipped through the alleyways of Venice, furtively making her way to the Calle Love of Friends. The streets were abandoned, the city asleep.

She had survived the fire . . . thanks to Peter.

Exhausted, injured, filthy, Oblivia wanted to control the doors at any cost, and she had almost paid with her life.

But now she was nearer to her goal than ever before.

Careful that she was not noticed, Oblivia entered the Calle Love of Friends. She entered a dark room in a secret house. There it was: the Door to Time.

Peter was waiting for her.

Oblivia smiled at him.

"Are you ready?" he asked.

"Yes, my love," Oblivia answered.

She reached for his hand.

Together, they opened the door . . .

What Lies Beyond The Door to Time?

When eleven-year-old twins Jason and Julia move into an old English mansion with their family, they discover a mysterious door hidden behind an old wardrobe. Together with their new friend Rick, they're about to unlock all of its secrets — and travel to places full of unimaginable mystery, and unavoidable danger.

There's a mystery in every masterpiece.

From the *New York Times* bestselling author **Blue Balliett**

A class project draws Petra, Calder, and Tommy into the mystery of Frank Lloyd Wright's Robie House. Tangled in a dangerous web, they must try to save the landmark— and themselves, too.

When a Vermeer painting is stolen, Petra and Calder are pulled clue by clue into a thrilling mystery that has stumped even the FBI!